I0604131

INTERVENTIONISM

DAVID J. WINTERS

{Subgenre:Publishers}

CONTENTS

ALSO BY DAVID J. WINTERS

Bedside Manner

Nurse-and-union-leader *turned* homicide-detective, Eminence Gray, uses her gifts of empathy and emotional labor to catch the most vicious of West Brandon's killers. Em's ability to maintain this skillset will be put to the ultimate test when the highest-profile murder case her department has ever faced falls right into her lap. Add to Em's troubles a corrupt executive from her union days, back and up to old tricks, and it might just be Eminence Gray requiring a little *bedside manner*... or a lot.

Interventionism
Copyright © 2023 by David J. Winters
All rights reserved.

No part of this book may be reproduced in any form or by any electronic or
mechanical means, including information storage and retrieval systems,
without written permission from the author, except for the use of brief
quotations in a book review.

*This is a work of fiction. All of the characters, organizations, and events portrayed
in this novel are too absurd for real life... except the elected officials and the
bureaucrats. Make no mistake, they're fictional. They just can't be depicted
absurdly enough.*

(A documentary, in aphorism, in 42 words...)

ISBN 9780991680320 (paperback) | ISBN 9780991680344 (hardcover) | ISBN
9780991680337 (electronic book)

{SubGenre : Publishers}
www.subgenrepublishers.com

$$1$$

IT'S THE FALL THAT'LL KILL YA

We're looking down on a forest, birds-eye. It's nothing so spectacular, just a bunch of poplars and the odd spruce sprouting up at us, some bluffs before the meadows, the usual. There's a defiance to that spruce though, mundanity notwithstanding, like it knows surviving the choke of the poplar monoculture is near impossible and it's beaten those odds. It gloats green for all our pleasure therefore. Green amongst the leafless lifeless sea of ashy mid-autumn pulp. It's pure mundane majesty until... *VOOOM!* A helicopter bursts into view obscuring *Mr. Majestyk* and the surrounding flora. The scene's a tabletop arcade shooter come to life all of a sudden.

A quick survey of the copter's cabin reveals five para-military operatives, all apprehensive-looking save for the stone-faced leader *Nand* and a cruel officious-looking *Newbie*. Nand has the stone face of a stone slab of a man—rigid, square, broad, serious from top to bottom—like you can trust this guy to get the job done *but what the hell job is that anyway?* Be careful where you point him. Newbie looks like an all-purpose toad. Grinning and appeasing-looking while at the same time able to stare right through the appeased and off in that direction for millions of miles. A scan downward from where Newbie crouches reveals a beige lump. The lump is a man, captive, keeled over on the floor like he's about to kiss feet. His hands are bound. His head is bagged. He's motionless. Nevertheless, the newbie hovers over him, minding him, periodically eyeing the captive and grinding teeth, devouring him bite by bite with his eyes.

Nand's engrossed in a GPS display, assessing something. A discernment washes over him and he looks up. He nods to Newbie. Newbie hops to it, initiating a routine that begins with removing the captive's wrist restraints. Next is the bag. An incongruity is revealed as it lifts. An incongruity in the captive's visage. It's apathy. Not a *resigned to one's fate* look of apathy or any such thing. It's more the look of someone sitting through an automatic car wash. Sitting somewhere between scrub and wax.

The captive starts muttering something only the newbie can hear if not understand. Newb leans closer to make out the whisper. He gets just within earshot as Nand pulls captive upright and away. Delicate about it too. Speaking of incongruous... He releases his hold the instant no conversation's possible. Force isn't needed anyway as the captive's relented to Nand's' admonishment-by-body-language. No more talk for the captive, he just kneels on the cabin floor, wondering if he even paid for that wax job...

The cabin door swings open and Newbie inches captive up to the threshold. Tilts him out the door by his shirt. Grip on the fabric's the only thing keeping captive from falling. At no point is there any resistance.

Newbie waits.

GPS device beeps.

Newbie lets go and the captive tumbles out of the helicopter. Gone.

Door slams. Newb turns to Nand for approval. Nand ignores him. Newb turns to the other mercs. They look at him like he's a man condemned. They cover the parts of themselves exposed to open air.

Newbie looks confused by all this for just an instant before... *KA-SPLAT!*

His internal organs, musculature, and skeleton explode from out the back of what's left of him. He simultaneously flattens like a pancake and springs like a fountain—in a microsecond. Newbie remnants are everywhere. Subordinates are displeased by the gore dripping off of everything yet none look surprised.

Nand's still business.

He turns to his Marlboro 100 smoking Second-in-Command, *Jane*. The gore explosion's left the Marlboro barely hanging on and we're not sure whether it's this latter circumstance or the former that's eating Jane most. Regardless, the displeasure's palpable.

Nand's not unsympathetic though there's an overriding pragmatism with him. "Two birds, one stone," he says.

Jane drags the cigarette back to life. "And a ride home in one of my dad's old hemorrhoids."

"So what ya want? Sit behind tarps?" Nand points to the remains. "Tip off *Faces of Death* here?"

"There's better ways."

"All putting us in the path of *The Gimmick*. This way's best." Boss leans back into his seat, a li'l loungy. Jane's expression's deadpan. A gob of the newbie at the tip of his nose plops onto his cigarette-holding upper lip. *PLOP*.

Nand's head cocks at this in the slightest. "...I'm open to suggestions."

"Throw the thrower," says Jane.

"No killing."

"Told ya, he's already dead."

"And I told you: *We don't do, what others do, where doing that gets people dying...*" Marlboro smoke blows in pregnant gesture. Nand watches it waft. "...*Fast.*"

Jane stops cannibalizing the newb and flicks his cigarette into the remains. *SZZZT!* "Psycho of the week explode slowly?"

"If a man, depraved, is gonna pull that trigger all goddamn day, least we can do is let him step in the path of his own ricochet."

A pair of manicure scissors trim two-thirds off the filter of another cigarette. Jane lights the lightable end. Takes a long drag. "The poetry don't boost efficiency."

"That's why we have The Gimmick."

2

―――――

PUTTING YOUR LIFE IN MY HANDS

The captive lies face-down on the forest floor. He's in a crater he made on impact. To be clear, we can only assume the body in the crater is his. An encompassing though dissipating glow obscures the finer details.

Just as the glow disappears completely... *WHOOSH!* It is him! He bursts onto his feet, alive as anyone. Not a scratch. Still apathetic. He's already running with a purpose if not direction. He runs through the bush, on and on and on. He's *Roger Jech*, the protagonist. A nobody as far as the world can tell just yet! He runs for yards, absentmindedly, right into a trip wire that topples him into a clearing. A flare goes off as he tries to get back to his feet. The flair whistles a piercing *SHWEEE!* as he rises. Over-armed soldiers pour out of the perimeter of the clearing, closing in on him. They're shouting in a verbal language other than his though in a body language that's universal: fear and distrust. They're on him now. Every single one of their guns pointed in his direction.

His apathy changes to concern *though* not for him. He

5

gestures to the soldiers. "No. No. English. English?" A leader-looking soldier responds by lifting his rifle a little higher. Jech waves his hands. "Please, no. Please listen."

He's staring down the muzzle of the leader's carbine now. The barrel's so close his eyes are crossing. From his perspective, it's like he's got railroad tracks coming out his forehead. Train tracks distract him for just a second though—*train* of thought indeed—and he's back to his imploring.

"English!?"

He's getting more and more animated. Can't help it. He's determined to get these soldiers to understand him yet all they see is an enemy invader completely unconcerned with his mortality.

He points at the leader with a *let's talk, just you and me* gesture. This only causes leader to put finger on trigger.

"I don't want to... I don't want *you* to get hurt." Jech pantomimes a man firing a gun. "You're all in danger." He points his finger gun at the leader who, as though not even realizing he's doing it, depresses his trigger micrometer by micrometer.

Jech continues pantomiming...

Trigger continues depressing...

When...

BANG!

Leader's passed that deadly threshold.

Shot ushers in others. All the soldiers open up on Jech at once. The countless overlapping booms of carbine shells popping their tops are deafening, blinding. It's all flash.

NAND STANDS HUNCHED IN THE helicopter cockpit, scanning. "There." He's pointing through the windshield to a slender mass emerging over the horizon. It's Jech. Alive again. Dispirited again.

As the helicopter hovers in place and stabilizes, we can see that Jech's standing dead-center a ring of prone bodies in perfect symmetry. The corpses extend outward for years. It's like an eye with dead men for an iris and Nand's mysterious asset for a pupil—fixed and dilated. The helicopter lands on the outskirts.

Jane and the rest of the mercs mind the helicopter as Nand walks out to our protagonist. Captive's hands stretch out to captor in a way habitual. At no point does Jech resist. If he looked at all tough, at all imposing, he'd give us the impression of a blood-soaked pit bull in a fighting pen, raising his chin for the leash. An act of strange docility that follows the tearing out of the throat of the opponent beast. But he's no beast? Bonds are put back on and Nand leads him to the helicopter. Copter lifts off and flies back to where it came from.

A NEW DAY—THE SOUND of the merc helicopter fades off into the distance. If we try hard enough we can *just* make it out sinking below a distant tree line. Then...

WHOOSH!

Jech bursts out of another crater and runs like he has time again. He runs and runs. He manages not to trip any alarms this time, making it to a lake. He assesses the natural barrier but doesn't want to linger as voices can be heard in the distance. He turns to the bush, then lake again, frantic, as...

A new day soldier appears out of nowhere. This one carries a substandard rifle. Rifle's pointed at Jech's midsection.

Cue the pleading. "English? English! Listen, please!"

Cue gun to Jech's face.

"Lis—"

No!

He stifles himself. Stifles damn near his whole essence. *No more.* He won't be killing this soldier, by soldier, in this bush. Not anywhere.

What we see now isn't apathy. What we see now isn't concern. Though it's something. Though he behaves it isn't behavioristic. Not a hint of mind behind it just muscle. Kinetics. Clumsy but determined physicality swiping for the soldier's gun. He gives it a smack to the left causing it to fire into the mud. *Keep going.* He grabs it by the forestock and pulls it forward, driving the barrel under his left armpit. Too much force. The gun breaks loose and goes flying into the lake as he falls backward after it.

Seeing him in the mud groping for the rifle, soldier pulls out a knife and prepares to attack.

Jech catches this and rolls supine. He wriggles, sitting up. He very deliberately shakes his head. *Don't you do it.*

Soldier doesn't care. None ever do. He commences slashing at Jech's midsection, missing. Too far. Soldier adapts. He switches from slashes to jabs as Jech, out of pure luck, knocks each attempt away. Frustrated, soldier goes back to a slashing stance, slightly telegraphing an incoming attack. He steps in, knife in a clenched hand of an arm cocked...

Jech cranes his head leaving his throat to the sky. Soldier adjusts his aim in light of the vulnerability. Goes for the trachea. *Trick worked?* Slash begins its arc as Jech opens his right hand over his Adam's apple. Knife tears across the open palm.

Blood wrings from the soldier's hand.

Soldier's?

Knife rolls out of oozing palm. Soldier's confused. In pain. Jech holds out his right hand revealing a glowing amber stripe where the knife had cut. Stripe fades revealing his palm's none the worse for wear. Untouched.

Soldier's palm isn't. He looks to it, gashed wide open in the same place Jech's had glowed.

Soldier comprehends.

3

ETERNAL RETURN REBUFFED

Again,
The helicopter hovers over Jech, standing in forest clearing.

Again,
Countless prone bodies circle him in perfect symmetry.

Again,
Helicopter lands.

Again,
Nand approaches.

Again,
Hands are outstretched.

Again,
Restraints come out.

But...
Hands go down.

"Put 'em on," Jech says.

Nand chuckles at the imperative. "For that you're going underground. For two days."

"Put 'em on."

"You make any move and we put you in that tomb for good. You think about that. You'll spend eternity underground with nothing but yourself and those lungs..." He pokes at Jech's chest. "...full of our dirt. I bet the despair's already sinking in."

"Not this time."

"Oh no?"

"No."

Like on cue the prone bodies rise, all their guns on all the mercs.

You'd swear old stone-face looks almost impressed by the ruse. "Clever," he concedes.

But Jech's not paying him any mind. His focus is across the expanse of rebels, at the other mercs. Nand may have entered this exchange unarmed, his men didn't. They aren't dropping their weapons.

Jane holds a net firing CODA, his other hand on a holstered single-shot sawed-off 410. Remaining mercs point m4 carbines. It's a solid stand-off between the mercs and the rebels. Nobody backing down. Jane's guarded if discerning. The other two mercs are neither. They're shouting naïve-macho slogans at the rebel soldiers who, pragmatically, shout back specific demands. Intentional divide notwithstanding, the two sides aren't speaking the same language anyway so the whole crew might as well be singing *Prisencolinensinainciusol.*

The rebels have the numbers. The mercs have the firepower—training too. Mercs would be toast in short order if the rebels pounced but they'd definitely take a dozen or so of the rebels with them. Add to this math a unanimous desire for self-preservation, and you have a perfect recipe for stalemate.

Then...

Game pieces scatter as Jech bursts through the vanguard. He's beelining it for Jane. All mercs but him point their muzzles as far away from Jech as possible. Jane is hesitant, net gun tilting up down up down as he deliberates. There's an agency in the gun, like it's reflective of the wavering deliberations. *Shoot, don't, shoot, don't...*

Coda wrenches upward. Jech's too close and getting closer. Net would just launch into his midsection, pulverizing any guts in its path. Wrenching likely wasn't necessary. Jane's grimace betrays the *why* of it: awareness of a failed opportunity is as good as lead weight on a man s'gotta move to relent. Jane does relent however, as Jech maintains that beeline.

CRACK!

He clocks Jane with strange animus, punch landing amateurishly. Jane shakes it off. That amber glow is back, fading from Jech's knuckles as he tries another swing. Jane maneuvers away. Other mercs just let this happen. Jech changes tack and grabs onto the net gun. Jane doesn't resist. Jech tosses it into the crowd—lets the mercs hold onto any lethal weapons. He paces back and forth in front of them. They keep their muzzles off him at all times.

Just keeps pacing, welcoming violence, when...

"Give 'em up fellas," Nand shouts from the mass of rebels. "He wants you to do it. He'd be more than happy to see you shoot your brains out at him."

Guns drop.

THE BUCOLLIA IS SO WELCOMING this time of year. Especially if there's one of those conceited spruce hanging around... It would be like a picnic if it weren't for the fact that it isn't. It isn't because—despite Nand, Jane, and the other mercs resting in the meadow clearing—repose is constituted entirely of men on their knees, hands tied behind backs. The rebels detaining them are doing so with shiny new M4s. They're visibly enamored with the tools too. Jane spits into the dirt in a gesture suggesting indignation. The less experienced mercs actually look kinda scared. Not what they signed up for?

And Nand? He's focusing on Jech, watching him negotiate with rebel soldiers off in the distance. He's watching him communicate mostly non-verbally. Jech appears to be getting his way for the most part though, curiously, when he isn't, when there's some kind of impasse, he stands firm using a familiar body language.

"*Stealing the culture of the empire?*" Boss says in hush. Now louder, "Just what do you think's gonna happen here Jech?"

A soldier reprimands this speaking out of turn by putting a thrusting boot between Nand's shoulders. Knocks him face-first into the sod. Jech's already walking toward as reprimand takes place. He closes the gap and, seemingly effortlessly, flips the merc back up and all the way onto his back without breaking any stride.

There's a slight glow.

Jech pulls Nand up to seated, gets in his face, "I think ... I think that what's going to happen here is, my new friends..." He gestures to the copter. "...My new friends, for that helicopter and the men responsible for decimating their people—"

"Army," Nand interrupts.

"What?"

"Only armies wound up dead. They weren't decimated either. They were *annihilated*. Civilians were unharmed."

No no no. You're not playing this asshole's game. Not in peace time. "Fucking delusion! Fucking delusion of yours, *not killing anyone who didn't deserve it*," Jech mocks.

"Not. Killing. Anyone."

"*They killed themselves*," he mocks more.

"They. Murdered. Themselves."

Enough language games! "Here's what'll happen. I'll be flown out of here and these men can do with you whatever they please."

Now it's Nand's turn to scoff. "You were saying something about delusion? Look around. Do these guys look like the soldiers that killed themselves killing you the last couple weeks? Those guys were better armed than we are." He points with his chin. "These guys have short shootin' .22s. A gun like that and a dead squirrel for lunch might get ya a dead squirrel for lunch." He catches sight of the rebel with the sliced hand now bandaged. Ears shift. Nostrils flare. "You're not curious about the anomaly?" Something other than calm is expressed in those last few words. "Enough. I don't want another second here. You fly away now and I'll meet the Premier upriver. Just get us out of here before the duck turns over."

Not this time! "This isn't ending with me obliging you," Jech lectures. "You're going up that river but you're getting your way like a guy in a guillotine askin' for a haircut's getting his way." He pulls a rag of torn shirt out of his pocket and stuffs it into Nand's mouth. "But you're not getting the last word."

With that, he sets out walking toward the helicopter... Confident... Definitive...

...As Nand opens his mouth *hardly at all* letting the rag fall out with ease. Merc shakes his head and's about to shout something though refrains. Jech wouldn't hear it anyway as he's now too close to the booming copter. Nand just watches his asset walk away, the last few clumsy steps of that asset transforming into a confident strut before taking flight.

All roles, of all involved, have been reversed in this bush.

4

———

RESEARCH

I t's six months later and we're auditing some sort of philosophy class. The class is in session at *Brandon West University*, a mid-nineteenth-century school in the town of *East Brandon West*. Professor *Toll Lytrall*, an academic looking to be in his mid-seventies, though otherwise nondescript, stands lecturing in front of seventy-five students of a class of two-hundred and fifty sparsely distributed around a four—hundred—person lecture hall. A glance around the room reveals the level of interest expressed on each student's face proportional to how close that student sits to the front. Few sit up front.

"So, to recapitulate..." Lytrall's placing an empty drinking glass on a seminar table as he speaks. "For many theorists, from Mill to Woodward, whatever a *cause* is it stands to reason that it must involve those circumstances such, should they not have happened, the *effect* would not have happened."

Professor swoops his right hand at the glass just hard enough to knock it off the table. The glass falls onto the linoleum with the intended *SMASH!* The more bored students startle back to attention.

"In this case, my hand played a causal role in the glass breaking because, all other things equal, *no hand swinging, no knocking the glass off the table, no breaking of the glass...*" He glances down at the clenched hand that did the damage. A small bead of blood runs out from the creases his index finger makes due the clenching. The running of the bead changes direction as he rotates his fist to get a better look. "...And no slicing my hand evidently." He tilts up at the class with an awkward smile. "My hand... Should take care of it." He issues his bloody palm toward the class to drive the point home. The few students up front appear disgusted. "Let's end a few minutes early huh? I Was just going to review the material for next week. You know how to read an outline."

LYTRALL EXITS THE MEN'S ROOM fanning damp hands. Professor *Glen Rice*—tall, stocky, imposing—intercepts him and puts a burly arm around his shoulder.

"How's the transition going ol' boy?" He reaches out reflexively, shaking Lytrall's hand, dragging him along down the hallway. "Heard you had a bit of an accident due your theatrics?"

Lytrall has a face like he's thinking *news travels fast.* "Some glass got where it shouldn't. It's like it never happened."

"Then let's act like it didn't. And the department?"

A bit of a beat... "Shouldn't I be teaching something closer to physics?"

"Ha! I'm a logician who got his start teaching ethics... For eight years! They'll put you in the right groove soon enough. In the meantime, the intro course gets you a week on science doesn't it?"

"Yeah, then three weeks on contemporary social issues."

"So?"

"So? They want me to talk politics in a humanities department at a legacy university. Why not have me talk options in a church?"

"You don't talk options here, you *are* in a church."

"I don't want to touch politics with a ten-foot pole."

"That's good because you're going to have to touch it with a five-foot pole."

"That's suicide."

"That's rigor."

"It's the 21st century!"

Rice stops the walk. "Believe it or not ol' boy, this department hasn't gone completely to shit yet. Some of us are still willing to drink hemlock. We have no use for faculty who treat circumspection as virtue and capitulation as responsibility. We ask the difficult questions here and when we're done doing that, the difficult questions about the difficult questions. You do that and you'll do fine."

Lytrall chuckles, shaking his head. "And what would you say the ratio of hemlock drinkers to hemlock pourers is these days?"

"Let's just say, *worse than yesterday*."

"And if I ask you tomorrow?"

"Ha! Perfect!" Rice reverts to his original boisterous self, starts leading Lytrall again. "It's questions like that that'll keep you doing just fine around here. Just fine." They walk a few more feet to Rice's office. Rice separates off and unlocks his door. "Well, this is me ol' boy. Got a meeting with a grad student trying to break the *law of non-contradiction* or something! Can you believe that? She's got balls this kid." He slams his office door before Lytrall can respond.

LYTRALL'S OFFICE IS BROOM CLOSET-like. It's a narrow space but there are high ceilings. The high ceilings make for high walls. High windowless walls. There are no bookshelves in this office either, or books. Unusual for any academic.

He sits, stares a second at the lack of dust where a computer used to be and takes out his smartphone. He turns it horizontal. "*Contemporary Social Issues*. Ok Toll, no point delaying the avoidable…"

A web browser displays the front page of the website *Spread-It*. Spread-It filters in content from all over the internet. It's mostly pop news items from major outlets and other ephemera, all dealing with subject matters users pretend to be very passionate about for a couple of hours before forgetting completely. There's pornography too. *And bubbles in beer… And sand in the desert…* You could call the website a *status quo aggregator* and be too close to the mark for the average user's tastes. A click on the search bar reveals a list of recent searches. At the top is *s/society*. Lytrall selects it. "*Research*." At the top of the s/society page is a link to a streaming video of a news broadcast. He selects that too. Why break with pattern?

On the screen, an anchor faces the viewing audience. He's formal in demeanor, over-serious, ridiculously coiffed, probably thirty-five but made up to look fifty… Literally every broadcast network anchor in the world for the last 70 years. He introduces a report that has since gone viral,

Over a dozen members of a local protest group are in hospital tonight after what can only be described as a vicious attack.

Members of the group WAMN were targeted outside an event held earlier today by the far-right extremist think tank, 'Friends of Noam Chomsky'. The fracas was far from your average street fight however, as the following amateur video shows.

A video superimposed over the shoulder of the anchor cuts to full screen. Its first image is a shot of a building across the expanse of a park. The camera operator pushes in on the building and a group of dark-clothed rioters comes into view. They appear to be harassing people entering the event.

Investigative reporter Simone Simmons—first name pronounced 'Simon'—is doing the reporting. The details of the video track her narration perfectly,

We see in the video several masked rioters throwing containers of fluid at event attendees. Some are even setting off explosives. Pay attention now to this lone pedestrian attempting to move past them.

The scene goes slightly dark with just a circle of regular brightness around the pedestrian.

A rioter tosses a lit explosive at an attendee and her small child. The pedestrian literally leaps into action, jumping in front of the explosive just seconds before it goes off. This gesture provokes the rioters who rush the pedestrian, surrounding him. And this is where things get very very strange...

The pedestrian is as difficult to identify as the rioters. Rioters wear identical uniform-like apparel, dark hoodie, black jeans, cloth mask. Pedestrian is in a black tracksuit under a raincoat, collar pulled all the way up to his temples.

He stands motionless among the rioters. He's still shrouded in the halo of lightness added by network editors.

The rioters are circling him when, without provocation, one of them, call him *Rioter 1*, rears back and shoves. Pedestrian is driven backward but at the exact point of contact, attacker flies off *his* feet in the opposite direction. Rioter 1's on his ass. Pedestrian glows.

Lytrall bursts up from his slouching posture. The telltale yellow glow hasn't just caught his attention, it's caused him to vibrate. He buries his face back into the phone.

Rioter 1's inciting shove has caused his pals to attack *en masse*. Pedestrian remains passive, absorbing various punches, kicks, and shoves thrown his way. Glow. Glow. Glow.

A couple more rioters—let's be extra clever and call them *Rioter 2* and *Rioter 3*—look to have hatched a little plan and move in on the pedestrian in lockstep. Rioter 2 and Rioter 3 punch him simultaneously, right jaw and left shoulder respectively. Rioter 2 and Rioter 3 are also affected simultaneously. Rioter 2 is spun to the left and drooling. Rioter 3's shoulder lurches forward and he loses balance. It appears as though this is happening due to some invisible force, always in the exact proportion of the damage inflicted on the pedestrian, always accompanied by that yellow glow. Various other rioters shove at him and are launched in the opposite direction too.

Rioter 4 is waiting patiently, cupping an iron bike lock hidden in a sock, hoping for a lull in the action.

Rioter 5 sees an opportunity, enters the fracas and boots the pedestrian in the knee. It's Rioter 5 who crumbles however. She's on the curb. Only knee damaged is hers.

Rioter 5's sacrifice gives Rioter 4 an opening. He whips the sock-lock a couple times in hand then swings for real, cracking the pedestrian in the back of the neck. Rioter 4 clearly makes contact though the instant he does it's he who collapses. The pedestrian can barely see the injured rioter as the most piercing glow yet has burst from where the lock made contact. Glow tells him the kid's hurt bad. Pedestrian spins, blinding the rioters behind. He crouches next to the kid. Kid's not moving. He reaches out but his attentiveness is cut short. The last remaining rioters have gotten their sight back and are moving in. They pile onto him.

LYTRALL IS SCRUBBING AND PAUSING the video looking for any frame that may identify the pedestrian. He peers into one of particular interest. Peering, peering, then unpausing. We hear Simmons again,

> *It appears the rioters have taken notice of the cameraman. We can only assume, due to the shakiness of the video, that the cameraman is attempting to flee as the rioters give cha-*

He locks the phone and leans back in his chair. Slight grin, big realization.

"Welcome home Jech. The prodigal son returns."

5

SIMONE (PRONOUNCED 'SIMON') SAYS

The *West Brandon Hospital Memorial Park* was established for West Brandon Hospital patients to get some fresh air and as a place to play for staff members' kids attending the onsite daycare. Establishing the park was a nice gesture but, in hindsight, it wasn't such a good idea mixing patients among large groups of children. Kids, with their germs, make sick people sicker and sick people, with their nearness to mortality, make kids kid existentialists—*viz.* less naïve existentialists. They bring the two groups out in shifts now.

Jech sits on one of the park's benches. He's arrived in time for the sick shift. He's pensive, observing a therapy golden retriever playing in a volleyball court. Really, *awash in the phenomenology of the dog playing* is the better way of putting it. Information is hitting his retinas but he's too lost in thought to attach any form to all the hue, saturation, and lightness. It's just skull theater. Doggie colors, volleyball court colors, hospital colors flashing unnoticed across the mind's eye. The dog could care less too. She's preoccupied with burying one of those rawhide bones in a hole she's dug. Until...

The tattered vestiges of the net above sway a little and spook her. She looks around suspicious, bone clenched hard in her mouth now. *No good! Not safe*, she must be thinking. Hole deep enough or not, it's time to bury her delicious dried-up bowtie of horse flesh where no one will ever find it. *PLOP!*

Jech stares in the direction of all this, as lost in it as ever...

WE'RE BACK IN THE POPLAR bush, in a large well lived-in camp. Sitting at the center of the camp is some heavy equipment, a hole it's dug, and a strange-looking apparatus. The apparatus is made up mostly of logs but there are several rocks tied to ropes hanging from one of those logs running horizontally. The horizontal log is propped up by a pair of sawbucks at either end. It's like a clothesline for drying stones.

Adjacent the apparatus is a hand truck anchored to the ground. Jech is bound to it, made to face the machinery.

"You get a good look?" says a voice circling around to Jech's front. Nand's still talking as he comes into view. "That there rig is our guarantee you don't turn on any of us or try to run the second we cut you loose." He points near the crane next the furthest sawbuck. "See that hole in the ground? See that bin hovering over it? Inside that bin is a metric ton of dirt, give or take a few kilos." He circles behind Jech again, releases the moorings on the truck and wheels it toward the hole. He continues explaining things as he goes. "We pull the pin on that container and boom! *That* ton of dirt fills *this*." he's stopped right at the hole's edge. He leans over Jech's shoulder and speaks directly into his ear. "Almost..." He tips the truck backward a few degrees, slowly. "See, there'll be about 160 maybe 165 pounds a' somethin' waiting at the bottom." He thrusts the truck forward near into the hole, fast, reels it out by chain. "Get it?" He holds Jech almost parallel the opening for a couple seconds then jerks the truck back vertical.

Jech breathes heavy. Heavier. He's on the verge of panic. Nand could care less about the plight. He's been banking on this reaction. He wheels the truck back a few feet so there's room for a face-to-face.

"You run, we catch you. Like we always do. Then you live in that dirt for as long as we decide to let you."

Jech rolls his head to his side, closes his eyes. *Gonna vomit? It'll get all over you no matter where you turn that head of yours. Shake him back... Bargain... Say something, do something... No! Defy him! Get tough ya bastard then push back as the bastard ya should be! Do it!...*

"Y—*you* gonna be the dummy gonna die pulling that pin?"

"The Gimmick?" Nand chuckles. "Well, that's the beauty of things. The beauty in the design really."

Merc walks over to the start of the apparatus. He takes out a pink, slimy, wormy-looking mass. It's pig gut. He ties a strand of it to a loop on a weighted pedestal surrounded by a shallow tub. He ties the other end of the gut to a hoop connected to a small thread. The thread's run through a hook above the tub and tied to a small rock. The rock is raised to the hoop by the thread he's tying to the gut.

Now it gets complicated...

The small raised rock has a slightly thicker thread extending from its other side. Thicker thread connects to a shear pin that holds a clasp onto a rope tied to a larger Rock.

Larger rock has a rope extending from its opposite that connects to a stronger shear pin holding a rope tied to an even larger rock... This goes on for about a dozen or so rocks, all increasing in size, and stops at the strongest shear pin that holds closed the door of the drop-bottom bin of dirt.

Nand smirks, pulls open a trap door flooding the tub with as many rats as there are rocks above. The rats immediately devour the pig gut snapping it. The smallest rock swings free breaking the first shear pin—releasing the second smallest rock shearing the second pin—releasing the third smallest rock shearing the next pin—and on through each subsequent pin until the last is wrenched broken and the half-ton of dirt crashes into the pit filling it instantly.

Heavy breathing again.

Nand moves back behind the truck. He grips the handles and whispers into Jech's ear, "I figure we can spare a rat or two." Truck's wrenched back into motion.

JECH STARTLES BACK TO THE present, bolting upright in his seat, eyes and face a red wash of vengefulness. *No more.* He smashes a fist onto the bench. This catches the golden retriever's attention. She bites into the sand gripping the buried bone and, in that covetous way that dogs protect their treasures, runs away.

Jech puts his glowing hand in his pocket, rises, and moves toward the hospital.

REPORTER SIMONE SIMMONS STANDS AT the door of West Brandon's ICU. She's talking to a ward nurse who's shaking her head like it isn't the first time she's done so this conversation.

"I'm sorry, I just can't divulge that."

Incidentally, there's a waiting room to Simmons' left. Her probing is of particular interest to one of its occupants. Jech sits in one of the waiting room chairs, eavesdropping.

"Can you tell me anything? At all?" Simmons tries. "Will he recover?"

Jech leans forward a little, angling his head toward the conversation.

"That's up to the patient to say," insists the nurse.

Jech sighs.

Simmons sighs. "Well thank you. I appreciate your taking the time."

"Again, I'm sorry I couldn't be of more help."

Nurse disappears back into the ICU as Simmons takes her phone in hand. She finds a seat a few down from Jech and sits. He catches himself staring at her so he smiles. He nods in addition hoping politeness negates suspiciousness. She smiles in response then goes back to her call. He's not convinced. *Idiot! Who ya think yer foolin'! She's on to you! Try again!* He decides on another tack. Maybe act like a fawning fan? You know, get her attention again and say *hey, aren't you on TV?*

"Hey, aren't you—"

"Excuse me ma'am," interrupts a janitor. "Do you have a minute?"

Jech turns away from the failed attempt at normalcy as Simmons looks up at the janitor. She gives him a once-over. *Nah.* She points to her phone in an *I'm busy* gesture.

Janitor persists. "I think I have something of yours you may have dropped... Back at my cart." He tilts his head toward the ICU door. Nowhere near any cart.

Simmons comprehends. "Yeah, you may be right." She gets up and lets the janitor lead her away from the ICU. They duck around a corner and into an elevator alcove.

Jech's not far behind. He slides along the wall to the corner just before that alcove. Inching his way up to it, he listens.

"You're that reporter wanting to know about the paralyzed kid?" the janitor asks.

"The public wants to know if he'll recover."

"*Right*. What's that information worth to you?"

"What's it worth to anyone?"

"It answers your questions."

Simmons opens her pocketbook. She looks to a wad of bills, then back to the janitor... Bills then janitor... Bills... Maybe she's gambling, maybe not. She takes out a fifty and issues it at the guy.

He appears half uninterested, half insulted. "Nobody I know uses cash anymore. It would cost me more to spend it."

"What do you want then?"

"I want you to say the name of my podcast next time you're on air."

Simmons frowns. "Can't do that. Regulations."

"Then no file."

"You ever watch the Carol Burnett show?"

"No one I know watches TV."

"No. Carol Burnett would tug her ear at the end of her show. It was a message to her grandma. It meant *hi grandma*. What if I tug my ear?"

"Grandma's dead."

"Tell your fans it means your podcast."

"My fans already know about my podcast."

"Christ! What's the name?"

"*My F*cking Podcast*," he boasts. Couldn't look more satisfied with that trite nonsense.

"That's what you call your goddamn podcast? Of course you put the fucking *f-word* in the title. I bet there's even an asterisk where the 'u' should be!"

He'd love to be indignant at this, but... "Terms of service..." he mutters.

"Well, our vulgarities are the last thing we'd want involved in any iconoclasm." Gives him a second. He fails to notice the contradiction. She decides on compromise. "I'll say it—no cursing. Best I can do."

"That's what gives it its edge."

"All the edge of a 10-year-old farting on an 8-year-old... How much edge does the asterisk get you?"

Couldn't look more deflated... "How do I know you'll really say it?"

"Cuz everybody says 'my podcast' all the fuckin' time. If you looked up *ubiquitous* in the dictionary there'd just be a note from Noah Webster sayin' *Hey! Check out my podcast*."

"I don't know..."

Simmons waves the bill. "Take my word for it or start saving so you can spend this fifty."

He relents. "You better say it..." Grabs the cash.

File folder opens. Simmons snaps a few pictures. Folder closes. Goodbye.

Jech barely registers the conversation's end in time to avoid the janitor. He breaks into a too slow *Hello stranger! I've only just walked up to this section of the hallway at a reasonable pace and am world-renowned for minding my own business...* walk-on-the-spot motion. Janitor doesn't notice Jech's attempt at appearing inconspicuous anyway. He's going to be a podcasting star doncha know... Janitor walks right on by, paying no mind.

In all his excitement, Jech's managed to move several steps backward with the brilliant pantomime. He inches back to within earshot of Simmons.

She's finally making that call. "Here's an update on that WAMN kid: 'paralysis caused by compression along C6 vertebrae ... Blood clot removed surgically ... Patient regained significant movement and sensation subsequent to surgery ... Prognosis promising'."

Relief washes over him. He's activated by Simmons' last statement. Time to leave... Carefully. He bolts for the ward stairwell. Simmons catches sight of him and his furtive demeanor as he slips away. She stares discerningly for just a second then gets back to her work.

6

PAYING THE RENT

The sandwich board on the sidewalk is as presumptuous as the sign above the door is obnoxious. The board reads,

Tonight: Single Elimination Super Swing Arm Wrestling Tourney! Entry fee $125. Grand prize $5,000. 8 buck cover. Two drink minimum.

In neon piping and flashing LEDs you'd swear account for every possible color of the spectrum, the sign over the bar door reads,

The Rio Bravo

IF YA THOUGHT THE OSTENTATION on the outside was extreme... We burst through the front doors of The Rio Bravo just in time to catch an announcer bursting eardrums. *I repeat! This is a single-elimination tournament. If you lose once, you're out!* A scan around the bar reveals college kids. There's a lot more neon inside too. It's your standard western-themed bar playing nothing but Top 40 pop. It looks fun enough. Keep adding booze to these kids' tanks and the fun won't stop until you spray it off with a hose.

Frat boys and jocks are drinking heavily, making themselves feel better after their tournament losses. They have upper body strength so they think they can win but they have no technique so they never stand a chance. They're generous and good-spirited losers though.

The tournament finals always came down to the same three football players. Two of the three alternating champs sit at a table sharing a pitcher of lager. The third, a cowboy hat-wearing fullback, stands at the plush vinyl pedestal where the wrestlers compete. He's made it to the final round. It's important to note that the tournament finals always *came* down to the same three ballers. Past tense. Not anymore.

Jech stands opposite the fullback at the wrestling pedestal. He wears a marathon runner's tag with the numeral '82' on it. He's dwarfed by the huge competitor staring down at him. The ball player is taking everything seriously but considering the swath cut by his opponent, has the face of someone not sure how seriously he should be taking it.

The two wrestlers get to their positions at the pedestal. A man in a Foot-Locker referee shirt stands between them. He puts his hand on top of Jech-and-jock's connected palms. "When I lift my hand, begin. You understand?"

They do.

Now, the way this works for Jech is: a little *push* on The Gimmick from his opponent turns into a *pull*. Opponent essentially loses by trying to win. It can't happen without some pull from Jech though, otherwise the crowd will notice the cheat. Just the right amount of push and pull and it'll look like our hero has exploited superior technique over brute strength.

It *would* if he could only keep his mind on the events at hand... He's gyrating his elbow trying to get it centered in the donut-like elbow pad of the wrestling pedestal.

Referee lifts his hand. *Game on!* but Jech continues to futz. He's absentmindedly putting too much resistance on the fullback's wrist as fullback gives it all he's got. Ridiculous amount of pressure hits Jech's forearm. Gimmick kicks in and the yellow glow slams jock's arm backward a million miles an hour in the losing direction. Arm hits the pedestal and breaks through the top with a *SMASH!*

Jech wins instantly.

There's a hush over the crowd. Vinyl, stuffing, and wood splinters are everywhere. The ref and the fullback look totally confused. Jech looks worried. Did he just give away The Gimmick?

Hush continues. Then...

The crowd erupts in cheers and applause. The fullback stares at Jech now less confused, more in disbelief, then breaks out in a smile himself. He puts his good arm around the li'l winner. "How the hell'd you do that boy? I mean, did I slip an' not know it?" Fullback raises his now tender competing arm. "Or're you just the toughest feller on earth? Either way I'm buyin' you beers! Name's Bob but everybody calls me 'Duckie'!"

Duckie drags Jech toward the section of the bar where the frat boys, sorority girls, and the rest of the team are drinking. Jech lets Duckie take him along in that direction too lest he risk betraying the secrecy of The Gimmick once more.

. . .

Jech's sitting alone now in a back booth. He's still wearing the marathon runner's 82 on his chest, Duckie's cowboy hat now on his head. A large novelty check for five thousand dollars sits next to him. A couple cordial glasses full of Jameson sit on the table too, fulfilling the two-drink minimum. He takes a drink of one and opens his mouth to let a little cool air in. An unanticipated glow beams due the whiskey-induced inflammation.

Glow catches the attention of an undergrad passing by. She's holding a drink in each hand and shouting inaudibly at some unseen entity across the room when the man with the golden maw becomes so much more interesting. She peers right into the glow, confused a second, then a look of realization like she knows exactly what's going on. She shakes her head, "Nice mouthpiece *raver*! You get that from my mom?"

She walks on. Jech's now glowless mouth goes tall-elliptical like he's making a *wuh* sound like he's thinking *well I never!* Now his mouth goes *huh* like he's thinking *how dare you missy!* He keeps bursting up then sitting in his booth, looking over to the kids each burst hoping they see his indignation and judgmental mouth shapes. *Let it go Jech!* Now his mouth goes-

"Can ya beat that! You can't be more than forty."

Simone Simmons has been standing outside his eyeline for a while now. He looks at her as though her presence isn't the most unpleasant of surprises which is foolish considering he knows she's been investigating him.

"I've been investigating you ya know? The *milquetoast vigilante*. You can deny it but that glow gave it away. That was you at the hospital yesterday too."

"Hospital?" he says, coy.

She breaks no stride. "All this time, I've been using your exploits for a story and you've been using my story for your exploits."

He scoffs. Playfully though. "Even if I am your vigilante, what does it matter?"

"How's that?"

"I've seen your reporting. You're the only one who seems to care about the guy. It isn't for your lack of trying to get others to care that they don't, but they don't."

"Then why not answer a few of my questions? Since it doesn't matter one way or the other?"

He's contemplative for a second... Resolve. "I'm gonna go over there and buy a pitcher of beer. Then I'm gonna come back here and drink a pitcher of beer. Join me if you want, but I make no promises of answering any questions. Or of getting you a glass." He drinks his second ounce of whisky. He covers his mouth with his hand again and breathes some cool air into it. Glow reflects off his palm and catches him in the eyes.

Ow.

SIMMONS HAS TAKEN JECH UP on his offer. A half-filled pitcher's on the table and he *was* kind enough to grab her a glass. He drinks his beer at a moderate rate. She drinks hers twice as fast. Talks faster.

"So what's your story? PCP?"

"Oh I'm not political..."

"You know what I mean. How is it you can just stand there taking those beatings? Or whip the cast of Conan the Barbarian in a goddamn arm-wrestling tournament?"

"On the record?"

"Of course."

He looks confused. "Is it *off the record*? Which one means you can't report on it?"

"Neither means I can't report on it..." She gets some sympathy in her eyes. "...But it's *off the record* that means I'm ethically obliged to not report on it."

"Off the record?"

"Sure."

"Well, off the record... It's irrelevant because *I'm. Not. Your. Vigilante*." He lets a little smirk slip.

She laughs. "You son of a bitch!" Laugh lingers in the smile to follow.

THE TWO CONTINUE TALKING. THERE are now two empty pitchers on the table and another half full. Jech's finishing some sort of anecdote.

"...It's like power of attorney, but for your ball sack!"

Simmons laughs uproariously. "You're disgusting!"

He shrugs.

A silence. Then...

"Jech?"

"Yeah?"

"What's your story?"

"I'll tell you on my deathbed."

"A guy who can take a baseball bat to the head like a cartoon... Something tells me I won't be getting you in bed any time soon."

He's taken aback a little. He'd do a spit take if this were that kind of a show. He's drunk, that's for sure, but did he just hear what he thought he did?

"*In* what?"

"Your deathbed. It'll be a long time before you're on your

deathbed."

"Ah..." He takes a big swig. Puts his glass down. She tops it up. He takes another big swig.

"How can I get your story Roger?"

"Pour me another?"

"Can you even get drunk?"

"Just don't pour it down my throat." He's slipping...

She grabs the pitcher, mimes a clumsy pour at him like she's going to do just that. Perhaps by accident, perhaps not, some beer spills onto Jech's hand. She begins dabbing at it with a napkin but she isn't attending to the site of the cleanup. She's looking Jech in the eyes. "Because what I do to you happens to me?"

Like he's losing at twenty questions... "Only if it hurts."

She squeezes his hand ever so slightly until... Squeeze turns into a pinch. Glow. He recoils at the exact moment Simmons does. A small pucker emerges on the back of her hand. She rubs it.

Jech's eyes open with a *shit-I-just-did-something-I-can't-undo* wideness. "Homina... *BURP!*"

Simmons grins back with a *what-do-you-think-of-my-journalistic-tae-kwon-do-now?* semi-wideness. Her expression turns wry.

He laughs. "*You* son of a bitch!" What else can he do?

He sits in the passenger seat of her car, outside his apartment. She looks at him with that same sympathy.

"Listen Jech, you never actually went back on the record tonight."

"I guess I didn't at that."

"You let me tell your story, I'll tell it straight."

A little wistful, "Like to know it myself." *It's not the worst of deals. Some seriously awful people already know about The Gimmick anyway...* "I'll think about it."

"Be sure to do that." Sympathy transforms to *juuust* a hint of a simper. "In the meantime, I'll be waiting... Waiting for you to play hero again."

7

THE FALL OF THE VIGILANTE

Jech reaches out to a scream. "You gotta try! It's goin'!"

Scream's the product of a window washer dangling from high from collapsed scaffolding. The back cable snapped from the outrigger above causing her cage to spill forward spilling her. She only hangs by miracle. No safety anchor, just the grip of a tiny girl in oversized coveralls with 'Ernie' on the name tag like she hasn't even been on the job long enough to get a uniform of her own. The rest of the rig is gonna go any second but the washer's too afraid to try for Jech's hand.

"Reach!" He thrusts his hand downward in a couple striking motions. *Come on lady, can't ya see my hand? Reach!* "Reach goddamn it!"

He loosens a foot wedged into a radiator valve anchoring him. Hangs out the window a bit further. He can see straight down to the street now. The awareness that he's never been so high off the ground while still attached to it hits him hard. He's woozy. *Pass out* woozy. He'd put his head between his knees but seeing as his head's outside and his knees aren't, head would have to go through concrete to do that.

World's going a little silvery around the edges on him when...

He feels a tickling at his fingertips. Washer's reaching up with her right hand attempting to take hold of his left. She fails to anticipate gravity's demands on her right arm however, triggering an instinct helpful under any other circumstance. Reflexively, she wraps her right arm back around the rail.

The attempt wasn't all for nothing. Her courage is enough to bring Jech out of his daze. "Keep your left arm wrapped around the rail and reach with the other," he orders.

She tries her best to follow the instructions. She braces her left arm around the rail and leverages against it, thrusting upward. Her right-hand stretches... Connects. Now she tries with her left. Another success! He heaves her upward with all he's got. Glow. The window washer rises.

Then... The *SNAP!*

The left-side cable of the washing platform breaks free from the outrigger above. The platform swings vertical to the right pendulum-like. Broken cable zips along with it. Flies downward with a wind-cutting force.

SCHWIP! The frayed end whips the window washer's wrists breaking her out of Jech's grasp. She plummets downward, falling, out of his sight. All we have left is Jech reaching down from the window of the monolith. Only this time he's not looking the hero just stunned. Eyes welling. Not ready to stop reaching. But...

He's lost her.

THE WINDOW WASHER FLAILS AS she falls. Piercing screams again. The excess fabric of her coveralls flap and flutter as the force of the air catches the cloth. She's supine but flailing, screams breaking periodically due the strain on her throat. It's heartbreaking though her trauma won't last much longer...

It won't last much longer because, despite the ground approaching rapidly from below, an unearthly yellow glow approaches faster from above. Jech, falling head-first, is piercing the air like a missile. He's catching up to the washer fast. As he falls just past her he grabs onto the shoulders of her coveralls, flipping her on top of him. They fall with Jech's back to the ground now. He stares into her eyes, demanding her attention. "When I say so," he shouts. "Shove me as hard as you can."

Washer tries to utter a *what?* but it's either the screams that stole her voice, the fear, or the sheer surreality. She can only mouth the word. Jech comprehends but they're approaching the ground fast!

"When I say *now*, shove at my chest as hard as you can. Both hands! As hard as you can! As hard as you—"

The washer begins nodding frantically. Jech nods back.

He glances to his right as they fall past a flagpole extending from the fifth-floor outer wall. Turns back to the window washer. "Now!"

He holds the washer as tight as he can at arm's length. She thrusts out against his chest as hard as she can. The Gimmick kicks in. Glow. Jech lets her go.

The force she exerts on him feeds back onto her and, in defiance of all physics, flings her upward at the exact moment Jech slams into the concrete with a glowing smashing *CRUNCH!* She flies four feet up and in the opposite direction of him, rolling to the side and landing as anyone would having fallen only four feet to the ground.

· · ·

LYTRALL IS HOLDING HIS PHONE, rapt. The tell-tale glow has once again caught his attention. The video he's watching is of a live stream of a live broadcast covering Jech and the window washer's fall. We see the glow he's left has swollen to a blinding intensity. Everybody on the scene is forced to look away. Cops, EMS workers, press, bystanders, everyone. When the glow finally subsides, Jech has vanished and we hear our familiar narrator:

> *Despite clearly seeing two figures plummet the entire length of the building, it's just our window washer who emerges from what can only be described as an ethereal glow. And, in defiance of all earthly explanation, she's emerged alive and seemingly unharmed. This is Simone Simmons, reporting.*

Lytrall tosses his phone onto his coat and leans back. "Reckless," he says shaking his head. "It's time to meet your maker Jech."

8

JUST GIMME THAT COUNTRYSIDE

He barges into the apartment, breathing heavy, muttering. He's as trauma-ridden as he was out there in that camp all those months back. *What the fuck was that!* He stomps toward the bedroom, pulling a non-mock turtleneck off himself as he goes. *What the fuck were you thinking!*

He drops the sweater on the floor just outside his bedroom and, heading toward the bed, starts tearing off wadded newspaper taped to his arms. *Mother fuck bucket!* He twists a motorcycle neck brace over his head, the kind motocross racers use to protect their neck and spine, and drops it on the bed. *They've always been the ones to throw you! You've never thrown you!*

The last thing he removes is a stab-proof ballistic vest that he bought for fifty bucks online. Maybe it works? *Coulda gone splat for all you know!* His chest is heaving at this point. He smashes his palm into it, *SMACK! SMACK! SMACK!*, until it and his upper body glow.

"What the fuck are you!"

He collapses into an easy chair. Sweat accumulates on

his brow as his breathing eases a little. He's clammy but calmed just enough to feel the bland discomfort of being too warm. He turns on his bedside lamp and leans in his chair, reaching to open the window. As he's reaching he notices something. A piece of paper taped to the top pane. On the paper written in large print is,

Outside.

Below 'Outside' is an arrow pointing down.

He moves down the stairs, taking in sensory information from all directions. Gets to the street. Street's desolate. The usual this time of night. Then, a voice...

Hey Jech...

It's coming from the alley. He peers inside. Maybe he should ignore it?

Hey man. Hey...

He looks like he's considering whether or not to ignore it...

Come on over...

Can't help it, he heads into the alley.

Dark dark dark... alley's dark. Jech moves toward the only object discernible, what could be a trash heap. It's a six foot tall mound, silhouetted, leaning against the wall opposite his apartment. Smells like hot sour jumping off cold puke. Likely garbage. Only light in the alley is a blink of an LED in the center of the heap. Not just garbage?

In here. Right here.

Heap's definitely the source of the voice. Jech approaches it.

He's fixated on the LED. *Flash! Flash!* Too much so to notice the shadowy figure sneaking up mime-like behind him. Cue the pizzicato *plink plink plinking...* The figure is setting up what looks like a hammock albeit vertical. The device is heavily anchored at the bottom. At least it appears to be judging by how gingerly the figure lowers it. Figure could drop the thing from the fire escape for all Jech would notice...

The LED has changed from a whispering voice to an intermittent beep.

Beep .... Beep .... Beep ....

He peers deeper into the light as the shadowy figure lets himself fall back into the hammock. Figure's sprung forward a little. His test's complete? Jech's still oblivious.

Beep ... Beep ... Beep ... Beep ...

Shadow rubs his hands together as he prepares to culminate whatever plan he's executing.

Beep . Beep . Beep . Beep . Beep .

Taps Jech on the shoulder.

Jech turns to the source.

It's Lytrall.

The Professor's pleasant enough, but that's about it. He's tipping himself backward imperceptibly... but pleasantly. For all Jech's marveling, Prof could be standing on his head.

Tipped sufficiently, he pauses. Then... Bursts forward at Jech shoving with all his might.

In perfect simultaneity, the pair fly apart in opposite directions. Jech lands in the trash heap that turns out to be a container of some sort, door slamming as he lands. Lytrall is sling-shotted out from the hammock back toward the container. As he flies we see his finger is pointed and fixed in some sort of anticipation. Lytrall's body moves through space but his hand, along with the rest of him, is perfectly still. The finger of the unmoving hand arcs along with the rest of the body in perfect trajectory, depressing a button on the container the instant contact is made. Container goes *DING!* like a microwave finishing a pizza pop.

Jech freezes in place, instantly.

Looks like it was a *tragic Jech trajectory* this whole time...

WE HEAR THE *WHOOSH!* SOUND expanding air makes as it leaves a smaller space for larger.

How is it you're smart enough to know to keep all this a secret,
but not scared enough to do it?

The container sits in a beautiful meadow. As beautiful as any Jech's ever been dropped. Maybe it's the season? The container door is open and Jech is as conscious as he was just before the *DING!* He's also lying in the only thing that's ever stopped him in his tracks. He bursts out of it gasping, barking human ignorance at it like a dog catching his leash on an electric fence.

"What is that thing and hand me a motherfuckin' baseball bat!"

Lytrall's standing by, a little insulted. "That *thing* is expensive."

"Expensive? *WHO ARE YOU?*"

"I'm Toll Lytrall. I'm here to help you harness your abilities."

"Why'd you bring me here?"

"Certainly not to help you harness your abilities..."

Jech didn't catch the sarcasm. He's too busy alternating between pacing and puzzling at the containment unit.

Lytrall takes a small fob out of his pocket. "Well this isn't calming you down any..." He presses a button and the meadow blinks out of existence. The context is now just slate with yellow grid overlay cross-hatching around a dome-like interior.

"What the hell is this a holodeck?"

"You think I brought you and that microwave to an *actual* prairie?" Lytrall scoffs.

"...Baseball bat..."

"No!"

Jech's reaching out. Not for anything to swing but to the wall. Does so without looking at it. *Not the slight bit curious Jech?* His face is aimed at Lytrall, its puzzlement in the process of being overtaken by indignation. His hand is still concerning itself with the wall however. Palm flat against the surface. It gives a slight push as though testing for integrity.

Lytrall reacts to the probing with a look of pride. "You are standing in *The Black Hole*," he boasts.

"Black hole?"

Look of pride transforms into one of *I thought you'd never ask*. Prof moves to the room's exit and opens the door, gesturing for Jech to remain inside. Jech obliges. Sort of. He grabs for the door ensuring it doesn't close. He's cautious, standing motionless, not sure if it's any safer *out* as it is *in*. What can he do? He stands pensive, observing what's going on at the other side of the door.

Lytrall's grabbed a bucket off his shop's workbench and is filling it with various small objects. Nuts, washers, a pencil, whatever's in reach. Done. He rushes back to Jech, bucket in hand.

"What are you—"

"I'm showing you my boy! Watch! The second I throw this bucket of junk into the air, I want you to close that door." He boots at the exit of the Black Hole a little. "Count back from one-hundred then open that door again. The second this junk is in the air, understand?

"How do I know you won't—"

Lytrall reaches for something outside, out of Jech's sight. Has it. Hands him a sledgehammer like he's a psychologist and not a philosopher all-of-a-sudden. Like he's a bloody clairvoyant. "It's not a baseball bat but it'll smash you outta here. But try the knob first..."

Jech chuckles so slightly.

Professor backs up and out the Black Hole again, nodding. Nods get a little slower like the nodding's saying *wait for it...* Then... He tosses all the bucket's contents high up into the rafters just like he said he would. Jech shuts the door. There's no discernible change in environment.

Come on man, got anything better to do? He begins the countdown.

"A hundred, ninety-nine, ninety-eight..."

. . .

"...THREE, TWO, ONE."

DOOR OPENS. No sledgehammer required. Incredible! All the junk that Lytrall threw in the air is exactly where it was a minute and a half ago. High up in the air, suspended in that instant between gravity losing and gravity winning. The stuff comes crashing down around a crouching Lytrall sheltering hardly at all under raised forearms.

Jech comprehends but in disbelief. Lytrall notices.

"Time doesn't pass outside these walls," he says bursting back into the dome, exercised as hell. "Shut that door and everyone on the other side of it halts." He shuts the door again to reify the point. "No movement, no aging, no processes at all. Time passes in here though. If I had anyone who cared about me out there, they'd have just lost ten whole minutes of me. They'd be losing even more time as we speak!"

Jech walks to the matte aluminum door of the complex. His shape reflects but is featureless due the dull finish. "And what about me?"

"You're in here with me. You haven't lost any time with me."

"No, what about the people who care about me? You think about that?"

The Professor mulls this over not at all. "With you it's no loss."

"Quite the people person..."

"You really have no idea what you are, do you?"

THE DUO EXITS THE BLACK Hole. They haven't exhausted its potential but its potential is more than implied. Good enough. Its exterior looks as you would expect. A convex compliment to the concave interior. What is striking however is the outer-shell's black-marble-like façade, smooth and glistening with just the matte door the only bland thing about it. The Black Hole's not insubstantial in terms of volume either but it is dwarfed by the facility it sits in. Place is poorly lit. Several of the high bay lights are off and yet you can tell the room's gotta be the size of an aircraft hangar. Space around The Black Hole is illuminated though. Lots of machinery is silhouetted back there. The portion of Lytrall's work-bench where he filled that bucket can be seen too. Shadow otherwise.

Jech takes all that's able to be taken in, in. "You a pilot or something?"

"It's for storing farm equipment."

Running his hand along the curvature of The Black Hole's smooth shell, "This don't look like a Hoyt-Clagwell to me."

"Farm went bust a couple generations back. These are just some of my proofs of concept. Theories in action."

"I'm in no position to care about any of this just yet and you know it."

Prof shrugs. "Why do you do what you do Jech? The hero stuff?"

"Pro arm wrestling?"

An expression of irritation, a corrective: "The milque-toast hero stuff."

"You mean vigilante stuff?"

Curious, "Now what kind of a man, called a *hero*, opts for less?"

"Heroes have courage."

"And you don't?"

"I've only taken two risks my whole life, the second mostly due to gravity…"

"Why do you do it then?"

"*With great power comes great responsibility*?"

"Ha! I got news for ya Toby, you don't have any power."

He don't realize it but he's been lulled into a conversation. He *does* realize this, he's quite offended by this rebuke. "The hell I don't!"

"Then do something powerful," Lytrall goads.

Specter of impotence affects our vigilante in all the usual human ways. He plants his feet on the ground like all he's thinking is he needs to prove this guy wrong. This perfect stranger. He leans forward, angles his cheek at him.

"Alright whoever you are. You want power, hit me… In the face… Hard as you can take it yourself."

"No."

"It won't work if you don't take a swing."

"*Noooo.*"

"Come on…"

"Look, I don't know what you think *great power* is, but last time I checked, it didn't involve gentle coaxing."

"Would you just take a fucking swing!"

Lytrall relents. "Alright alright. Just… Let's be mindful of the equipment, huh." He gestures for Jech to move away from The Black Hole, to where his workbench meets shadows. Jech moves along with him, real impetuous. *Let's get on with it!* The Professor motions for him to stop. They're in the right place evidently.

Jech still stands with his face protruding.

Lytrall poses like a boxer, albeit theatrically.

Another device begins to beep. Something's happening. *Beep.*

Jech cranes his neck backward. Nothing there.

Beep. Beep.

You're gonna have to do better than that...

Beep. Beep.

"I'm not falling for this aga—"

BOOM!

Out from the dimly lit workbench, a robotic arm cracks our hero in the chest with a bajillion pounds of force. Swung faster than human perception. Arm flings him across the facility, smashing him into the rear wall.

CRUNCH! Glow.

He isn't hurt but he's sure crumpled. He struggles to get up as Lytrall approaches, hovering.

"My god! Step lightly mighty champion lest your tremors crumble the highest mountains!"

Jech jumps to his feet. "You should be dust."

"I didn't do anything. The arm did. AI."

"Then *it* should be dust."

"Not how it works Jech. You should know that."

Jech looks like he doesn't know that. Lytrall notices, sighs.

"There's only The Gimmick if 1. there's any damage, 2. the entity inflicting the damage is organic, and 3. the entity makes a choice to do something immediate where, if that something wasn't done, there wouldn't be damage."

A contemplative pause from Jech. Then... "Who are you?"

"Your maker. Right here." He gestures all around. He hits another button on his fob and the remaining lights come on. Facility's full of high tech but the function of any of it sure isn't clear.

9
____

BACKSTORY

Imagine Woodward and Bernstein's office from *All the President's Men*. That's Simone Simmons' office in a nutshell. Open concept, desks butted up against each other, only a lot smaller than the sprawling office floors of the movies. Simmons sits at one of those desks adapting some copy to script for her next segment.

A man in a suit and dark glasses approaches her. *Suit-Man* gives off a formidable enough air but also one of a medical supply salesman. Think, a used car salesman if used cars kept you alive.

He observes Simmons' nameplate then taps a finger on her desk. Says each syllable of her name with a tap. "Sih-moan Sih-mahns?"

"*Simon*" she says, noncommittal.

A glance at the guy and her expression changes from preoccupation to one of recognizing an actor you never talk to if you don't have to. There's deliberation a second, then... She shrugs a *well, get on with it* shrug in his direction. Doesn't utter a word.

He smiles an empty smile. "Ha, I get it! Never be the first to speak in a negotiation…"

"We negotiating?" she relents.

"Can we?"

"No."

"Ah, *just a little?*"

"*Touché.*"

"Gotcha!" He laughs. Acts like they're friends now. "You've been investigating one Roger Jech?"

"Nah. Too busy investigating our local vigilante."

"Oh yeah?"

She's mum again.

Suit-Man turns off the faux playfulness. "You can cut the shit whenever you want Simmons." He tosses a couple pictures of her and Jech onto the desk. The pictures were taken at the Rio Bravo.

"Drinks with a friend doesn't constitute an investigation."

"He's dangerous Simmons."

"Scourge of the undergrad arm-wrestling circuit…"

"I'm going to do you a favor. The following information is privileged, so my providing it is a matter of grace on my part. Government grace. The best kind of grace. Ever hear of the *London Culling?*"

A little less flippancy, "All reporters have."

"Hardly any eyewitnesses. Know the one consistency in their testimony?"

Drops the irony completely. "No."

"Yellow glow."

"The London Culling was 45 years ago. You saying the vigilante is over 65 years old… And Canadian?"

"There's the investigative reporter we all know and love!" Suit-Man is back to acting like he's talking to a cherished friend. "I'm saying Roger Jech is the vigilante and that glow is no coincidence."

"Speaking of *saying*, my gramma had a saying, *one grain don't get you gravy*. Not only's your story thin, it's contradictory. The vigilante's a pacifist."

"Just because he doesn't throw a punch doesn't mean no one gets hurt."

"Never killed."

"*Yet*. Regardless, he's breaking the law."

"So call the cops."

Not so friendly again, "That's fine. You just keep fraternizin' with Roger Jech. I'll be back to get any information when ya do. Whether by *film at eleven* or subpoena."

"We don't use film anymore."

"And we don't use subpoenas."

JECH AND LYTRALL WALK ACROSS the large homestead toward a farmhouse. They're mid-conversation. Lytrall's playing the didact.

"...Quantum zeroing. A phenomenon a colleague and I expounded on a few decades back. Highly applicable too. Every one of the particles in your body is designed to be attuned to every other particle in the universe through *induced quantum entanglement*."

They get to the door of the house. Lytrall unlocks it, opens it, then turns. He points to Jech's chest.

"You're invulnerable. Immortal. Somebody damages the cells of your body, the particles in those cells instantaneously bind to like particles. Like particles get converted to energy and then back into the building blocks of matter needed to repair your damaged cells. Problem is, that energy has to come from somewhere. That *somewhere* is the person who caused the damage. Understand?"

"Yeah, yeah, *midichlorians*..."

Lytrall slumps a little at this. "The coldness of space will kill a man dead. Never quicker than when in his head."

Jech gets the disappointment. "Look, I'm all for education, but explaining to me *how* I function tells me nothing about *why* I function, you know?"

Prof comprehends. A pause. A decision made. "I've got one last thing to show you."

WE'RE LOOKING AT A RICKETY wooden shelving unit. The shelves hold several glass jars. The contents at this point are just amorphous blobs in colored fluid. Jech's face is pure horror.

"What are those? Failed *mes*?"

"No!" Lytrall yanks a string attached to a bare lightbulb, illuminating the jars. "They're stewed tomatoes."

Stewed tomatoes sit on the shelf of what turns out to be the farmhouse cellar.

"Except for those... Those are beets..."

Some canned beets sit on that same shelf.

Lytrall steps into the center of the room and stomps his foot. A one-dimensional laser line begins scanning the length of his face, top toward bottom. The beam hugs every contour, causing his eyes to strobe and flash as it moves along them. Beam continues the scan until finally dripping off the bottom of Lytrall's chin and on into oblivion. The patch of floor where the two stand begins to descend.

. . .

IT'S JUST ANOTHER FACILITY FULL of tech, only smaller. Pristine silver surfaces make up the bulk of the three-hundred-fifty square foot room. The only recognizable device is another containment unit. Jech notices it right away.

"I'm not in the mood for a nap."

"Too crowded."

Lytrall flicks a switch. The inside of the unit is illuminated. A figure comes into view behind the glass. The duo, shoulder to shoulder, lean in to get a better view. Looks like a corpse in a beer bottle.

"Meet your counterpart."

"There's two of us?"

"Between the two of you there is."

What's this guy really up to? Jech turns to The Professor, moves forward, no stopping.

Professor knows to back up along with his flow. *Show him your belly... He doesn't yet trust...*

He's imposing on Lytrall now. "Alright, enough about me. Why do *you* do what you do?"

Prof knows to oblige here too. Begins explaining things like it's the easiest tale to tell in the world: "Unlike you, I do have great power... Give or take a watt." He gestures at all his equipment, then to the man in the bottle. "Imagine a world with just the right number of *Roger Jechs* in it. All you guys need do is merely exist, just *be*."

IMAGINE...

A MUGGER RAISES A GUN to the back of an unsuspecting victim's head. *BOOM!* Glow erupts from the intended victim's forehead but it's the front of the gunman's head that explodes. Vomits brain all over the back of victim. Gunman goes down revealing three accomplices behind him. They're confused, frightened. They run.

Who'll pull a trigger for a pocketbook if it might be his own skull he's blowing open?

Mugger snaps back to reality. Has a look of realization. Drops the gun.

IMAGINE...

SOLDIERS ARE MOVING THROUGH SOME non-descript jungle when... Ambush! Triggerman in a machine gun nest opens fire on a soldier taking point. Soldier's chest erupts in glowing beams.

Elsewhere, a bureaucrat or politician or both is sitting at his desk, chest bursting with dozens and dozens of artillery punctures. Blood sprays everywhere. He collapses, exit wounds smoking.

Who'll send even a single man to war if it means making himself cannon fodder in an office chair?

Bureaucrat snaps back to reality. Has a look of realization. Drops the pen.

IMAGINE...

A SMALL UNASSUMING CITY RESTS peacefully off in the distant horizon when... *FLASH! BOOM!* A mushroom cloud erupts within it ending the municipality in one vicious second. Elsewhere, a war room bunker's worth of politicians, military officials, and bureaucrats turn to vapor.

Hell, who'll push that button if it means reducing himself to dust?

Hawks snap back to reality. Have a look of realization. Drop the football.

. . .

LYTRALL'S DONE PLAYING BIZARRO JOHN Lennon. Time for the upshot... "I figured, put enough of you guys out there in the world and boom, peace and harmony."

Imposing eases. Jech shakes his head, incredulous. "You underestimate a man's ability to exceptionalize himself. *When I pull that trigger things will be different.*"

"Well your enemies are proof of that." He nudges Jech aside, moves closer to the container. "I thought I was lighting candles in the dark. Put enough of you guys out there and... *Where your light shines, darkness recedes...*" He gets a little singy-songy with those last few words. "But..." Lightheartedness fades quickly, "...Just one of you decides people are *means* to your ends and not *ends* in themselves, you'll eat a hole through the world."

Jech points to the beer bottle. "Him?"

"A fuse is as good as a wick in the dark." Lytrall mimes the expanding of a mushroom cloud while mouthing the word 'kaboom'. "He called himself *Crimson Dawkitt*. He put one of those holes in the world and he was still chomping when I caught up with him." He taps on a row of LEDs next to the container. Whatever the tapping achieved, it satisfies him and he moves back to the other side of the laboratory. *Enough time spent next to the man in the bottle?* He leans against the counter to rest, speaking as though without audience. "I keep Crimson in here because I once made the mistake of letting him out there. If an old man's guilt could bind him, hell, a cage at the center of the sun would be less confining. Who knew people with your gifts could be psychopaths..." Exhales from deep, "*If only* a man's guilt could—"

"I get it..." He's talking to Lytrall but facing Crimson. "...

I'm here because you need someone, just like him, to deal with him."

"You're here to get a handle on your abilities. So you can have a life."

Turns to The Professor now. "But you think I owe you for that life?"

"More like I think, one day, you'll choose *hero* over *vigilante*." Prof lifts himself upright from the counter. Now it's his turn to impose. "I know why you do what you do Jech. It's the only reason in the world for people like you. Pardon the equivocation, but you crossed paths with a monster so cruel it broke the unbreakable. If they can do it to you, they can do it to anyone. So now you're determined to stand between every monster and the world."

He's shaking his head at Lytrall for some reason, like of contrarian reflex. He's prepared to contest every hypothesis, only... Thought creeps in.

There's not actually anything inconsistent about what he's said Jech...

Consistency isn't truth. There must be proof...

They're your intentions. Either you intend this or not. Well?

I...

"I..." He smiles. *Nail on the head.* He nods at Lytrall. Lytrall comprehends.

"Right. Now we need to get you into shape."

10

MOMENTARY MONTAGE

It's a large metallic cylinder. Lytrall unfurls it like it's a roll-up gun bag hanging off an old nag in an old western. He pulls devices from it. Devices sure appear gun-like but of a strange semi-transparent material. Like a bottle fly's thorax. What we see are the following. A pair of bottle fly Glock 19 pistols, a bottle fly Colt M4A1 carbine rifle. There're also black gloves, the fabric of which is like fine pumice. Prof picks up the Colt and bounces it in his hand. He looks very proud.

"The guns fire high velocity electrically charged plasma. The gloves eject the same on impact. Immobilize an elephant, never hurt a fly. Look at this..." A button on the Colt is depressed and the shooter extends transforming into a Heckler & Koch PSG1 sniper rifle. "...For long distances." He depresses the button again and the PSG1 contracts back into the Colt.

"What'd you rob NASA or something?"

"You think the public sector could come up with this tech? First things first. Here." He puts what looks like a bottle fly-skinned Tylenol in Jech's hand. "Swallow this and I can track you wherever you go, in case you get in over your head." Goes somber a second. "There are obvious downsides, so think very carefully before taking it."

Jech pockets the pill.

Lytrall gives him the Colt. "How's it feel?"

"Light." He tosses the gun without letting go.

Lytrall hits his fob. An anthropomorphic creation of his bolts out from the dark sprinting toward the pair. Prof steps aside and The Creature keeps on its path. Creature's coming for Jech. Thing's very swift, very agile, very *bottle-fly-like* in its armature, and it's bearing down on its target closing that gap.

But Jech's aware! Alert! Prepared?

Quick as a flash he does nothing. The mechanical man clobbers him with ridiculous force and our hero flies across the facility.

Lytrall ambles up to the crumpled glowing heap. "Was the safety on?"

Jech props himself up onto his elbow. Winces in The Professor's direction. "Safety?"

"Try again."

He's barely to his feet and Lytrall's at it again with that fob.

A second mechanical man emerges, running at Jech like in replay. *Not this time!* He aims the Colt at the charging mech trying to get the attacker in his reticle when...

BOOM!

The first mechanical man clobbers him from behind. Forgot he was there. He stumbles forward. Glow. He turns to aim the Colt at the mech behind when...

BOOM!

The second still charging mech clobbers him from a *behind* that was just moments ago a *front*. Forgot about this guy too. Round one retread. Jech flies across the rest of the facility right past The Professor already walking in that direction.

Lytrall hovers. "Didn't even get a shot off. This is going to take a lot longer than I thought."

PAIR STANDS NEXT TO THE Black Hole, Lytrall looking real proud at everything once again.

"The world doesn't have the time to make you a hero. Lucky for you, there's nothing but *time* in here." He opens the Black Hole door and gestures that Jech should enter. "Now go get it done."

"And how exactly do I do that?"

"I thought you might ask. Here." He hands Jech a couple pounds of dubious hypothesis: *Outliers: The Story of Success*. "10,000 hours and you'll be able to shoot the Y chromosomes off a sperm cell."

Vigilante's dismayed.

Professor realizes something, shows all due concern. "Listen, you're gonna be in there for a long time, maybe years. That could make you go loony. Better take this too."

He hands Jech a copy of *Introduction to Psychology*.

"Thanks..."

"Ready?"

No less dismayed, "Sure."

Lytrall nods.

MONTAGE TIME: MEATLOAF'S "OUT OF the Frying Pan (And into The Fire)" swells.

Jech slams each Glock into his hip holsters. *SLAM! SLAM!* He clicks the M4/PSG1 onto the magnetic holster on his back. *CLICK!* He slides the gloves on. *SLIP! SLIP!* He approaches the door of The Black Hole stoically. He looks in, then back to Lytrall. He gives a thumbs up. Lytrall gives a thumbs up back.

Jech enters... ...Exits instantaneously.

Meatloaf song cuts out abruptly.

"A minute and a half?" Lytrall's assessing a digital readout above the door of the Black Hole. The readout—appearing as though behind the black marble—indicates the time Jech's spent inside. Says *00:01:29*.

"I'm really immortal?"

"Damn it Jech!"

"I'll be in there a long time."

"You'll be out here longer you keep leaving every time you feel the slightest doubt at the impossible. To have me prove some existentialist's infinity for you."

"Huh?"

"If you're immortal there's always going to be another moment lived after any other. That's *an infinity*. How can I prove there'll always be one more? It's an induction that never ends where to carry it out requires a step that says: *there's always another moment after a next*, but that's precisely what it is to live forever! To prove you immortal I'd had to have first proven you immortal where I'd had to have proven you immortal to do that... but I'd have proven it before that *before* too... and on... all the way back to, of course, infinity.

"Hell Jech, in terms of certainty, I can't even say you'll be alive the instant I finish this sentence though I've seen you fall off a forty-story building and walk away, heard stories of you taking more bullets to heart ass and face than a country-road stop sign, of you spending a week buried ali-."

"Invulnerability *now* doesn't mean invulnerability *forever*."

"*Still kicking...*" he mutters. "That's what I've been trying to tell you: nothing is certain."

"I'll be in there a long time."

"I've seen you sleep in a bottle for years and not age a day. Be nice if I could say the same for myself..."

"Where's the proof?"

"No proof, abduction."

"Don't I know it."

"Not that kind of abduction. *Best explanation.* There'll be no waste of life. Trust me."

"I'll be in there a long time!"

Prof sighs. "I was hoping I wouldn't have to resort to this..." He hands Jech a copy of *Outliers* in audiobook format along with a Discman. "Abridged. Satisfied?"

Meatloaf's "Out of the Frying Pan (And into The Fire)" swells once again.

Jech gives a thumbs up and reenters The Black Hole that he exits right now.

Song cuts out abruptly for a second time.

"Alright, let's see the talent." Professor hits his at-this-point all-purpose fob. Three mechs dart out at Jech from the shadows.

Jech draws one of his Glocks and hits all three from the hip. *BIM! BIM! BIM!*

"Not b—"

He pushes Lytrall aside and whips out the Colt, transforming it into the PSG1 as he aims. *BIM!* He hits a fourth mech square in its bottle-fly head. The armed automaton falls from the rafters at the far end of the facility.

"—ad. Ok, paid off! And it only took you…" Lytrall squints at the readout. "…18 years! You didn't happen to become expert at 14.768 other things while in there did you?"

Jech's dismayed again. Lytrall notices again.

"No worries. Skills are there. No need to—" he punches at Jech who quick as a flash does nothing. *CRACK!* Fist smashes nose. Professor recoils grabbing his face, covering it with his palms. Blood seeps from those palms as Jech's face glows.

Lytrall stumbles backward. "Jesus!" He keeps stumbling. He arcs himself in a circle looping back around to a Jech trying to see through his own glow. He speaks through bloody fingers at him. "What are you going to do if someone takes a swing? Get back in there!" He points at The Black Hole with one hand now, pinching his nostrils closed with the other. "Don't leave until you can handle yourself."

"You okay?"

"Get in there!"

Jech tugs his gloves tight. Meatloaf swells. He reenters without hesitation… …Exits. Music stops.

Lytrall's still holding his bloody nose.

"You a hemophiliac or something?"

Prof doesn't grant Jech the dignity of a response. Just hits his fob with his free bloodied thumb.

A dozen or so mechs charge. All but one come at Jech employing a different martial art. Mech not fighting just stands by. Jech takes the attackers on hand-to-hand. It's some krav maga/kung fu bullshit unlike any movie has ever depicted! Looks ridiculous yet damn if it isn't effective! He dodges and counters and then fucks up near all of Lytrall's mechanical men. All except *bystander-mech* collapse from his blows.

Lytrall approaches the aftermath with bloody tissue hanging from each nostril. "Not him?" He points at *Bystander*.

"Didn't attack."

A nod of approval. "Time for you to go to work."

Meatloaf song starts one last time.

Prof holds out an open palm gesturing to Jech for a high-five. Jech obliges. They high-five! Freeze frame on palms together, glow emitting from them.

Into the fire! Fire! Fire! And into the fire...

11

RISE OF THE HERO

SEQUENCE I.

We're on one of the streets of uptown West Brandon. A row of Greystone houses and apartment buildings sit chock-a-block all along it save for a vacant lot near the center. The mercury vapor lights outside the lot venture in about two-thirds the way before losing their nerve, leaving nothing but darkness from lack-of-nerve on. Block looks like an invisible fist's knocked a tooth out of urbanity, leaving urbanity to ask *what, me worry?*

A woman walks her dog along the block's sidewalk. She's frustrated in a way any dog owner will recognize: poochie's gotten her out of bed at two in the morning whining like the Pacific's about to pour out of him only to drag her around the neighborhood sniffing parking meters. The dog is a large and hugely pleasant black lab. The woman is slight yet pleasant herself. We can tell she's pleasant because, despite her frustration, every time she glances down to her dog sniffing—only to have her hopes of evacuation dashed—she can't help but grin at him lovingly a second or two. She grins the tired grin of a woman at the whims of a bladder that's gonna wiz when it's gonna wiz but it *ain't* gonna be all over her living room floor.

Her frustration causes her preoccupation and her preoccupation keeps her from noticing she's on a collision course with a man talking on his phone. It's not for the man's lack of trying either. He's talking quite loudly, almost theatrically. As their paths cross, he turns, bumping into her, simultaneously dropping his phone and getting wrapped up in the leash. He stares at *Dog-Walker* with a stern displeasure, then, working against the tangle of the leash, bends to pick up the phone.

His expression transforms into an artificial smile as he lowers.

"Sorry," he says, locking eyes with her.

"It's ok," she offers meekly, looking upward and away to avoid the odd stare.

The man reaches in the direction of the phone. He doesn't break from the stare at all except to examine the location of the dog's leash relative his hand. *CLICK!* He grabs his phone and rises.

"Got it," he says, waving the phone.

Wave wave, tweet tweet... The tweeting sound echoes from the vacant lot. The dog bolts for it as Dog-Walker realizes too late the leash has been detached. It's all reflex for her now. She drops the handle of the leash still wrapped around the man with the artificial smile. Runs after her dog, calling for him.

SHE ENTERS THE ALLEY, STILL calling as she goes. The dog barks from the shadows. She calls louder. Out from the shadows he comes, a man leading him by the collar. The man moves himself and the dog closer to the woman, an obvious menace about him.

Dog-Walker's eyes well up. She backs away, reaching out for her dog, mouthing the word *come* as she leaves. Dog doesn't. She bumps into something. It's the man with the artificial smile. He grabs her. Dog barks again as the *Menacing-Thug* wrangles him. "Shhh."

Artificial-Smile covers the woman's mouth as Menacing-Thug does the negotiating.

"Relax. Don't want to hurt you or the pooch. An' we won't, long as you give us what's in da purse."

Smile removes his hand from the woman's mouth so she can respond. She's frozen. He nudges her, points to Menacing-Thug. "Answer 'em!" he demands.

"I—I don't have a purse..." she relents.

"Too bad," mocks Menace, "But you heard the options. We gonna start with you or the dog?"

The two goons laugh. They laugh in a way they need their victims to fear... The kind of laughter you pray never ends because once it does only the unimaginable may follow... And, with these guys, the unimaginable *will* follow. Unless...

SWOOSH!

A streaking, tearing flash erupts from the entrance of the lot. It's proceeded by a low rumble, then a tremendous glow. The glow neuters the gloating cruel laughter within the lot...

Smile turns himself along with Dog-Walker to the source of the disruption. What the two behold is a man, kneeling, wearing a winter face-warmer riding up to just below his piercing eyes. Shortish hair nearly flows from out the top of the warmer. The masked man rises triumphantly, bathed in aforementioned glow. It's Jech by the way.

Smile watches on, less intimidated more confused. *What's with that glow?* The confusion causes his grip on Dog-Walker to loosen and she takes advantage, wrestling out of his grasp and moving away. Smile just lets this happen. He's not taking his attention off this new threat. Whatever skills of deliberation he possessed must have been exhausted on that leash-cutting trick as all he can do now is cock his fists and move in for the attack. Menacing-Thug thinks the same. He lets go of the dog's collar and moves in to assist, unfolding a buck knife as he goes. Smile gets to Jech first and...

WHIFF! WHOOSH! Jech ducks and weaves around Smile's blows, nonchalant as anything. *WHOFF! WAFFLE!* he keeps keepin' Smile from landing a single punch as Menace jumps into the fracas, taking a swipe. Jech anticipates it, grabbing and bending Menace's wrist in one fluid motion. Knife flies from Menace's grip and into the penumbra of the dark. The same dark Dog-Walker and her lab shelter in, reunited. Walker takes the knife, folds it into its handle and pockets it. *For next time?*

Jech tires of all the dodging. *What's the point of The Gimmick if you're not going to use it?* He goes still. The two goons waste no time. Smile goes right for the cheap shot, kneeing Jech in the scrotum. We all know what happens next. Glow beams out of Jech's crotch as Smile crumbles, hands-on-groin, writhing blue and clammy on the ground. Menace has picked up a one-by-four slat in the interim. He swings it and connects with Jech's face right at the left cheekbone. A glow emits from that cheekbone at the exact moment Menace is spun around by The Gimmick, twisting him at the waist. Menace's face looks anodyne, his eyes roll back. He goes down, cold.

· · ·

MENACE AND SMILE SIT ON the sidewalk in front of the greystones, back-to-back, dazed, hands zip-tied around each other's.

A police cruiser pulls up. Cop from the passenger side exits and surveys the scene. Starts interrogating. "Alright," he says to the thugs. "What happened here? Which a you two saw something?"

The driver's side cop assesses the two muggers. "Looks like this guy saw something..." He tilts Menacing-Thug's head to the right. "...All three-hundred-sixty degrees of the truck tire that ran over his face."

Passenger cop's not in the mood for jokes. "Come on! Who saw it?"

"Officers, I saw what happened." Dog-Walker emerges from the entrance of her apartment building, a portion of her meekness replaced by a sense of justice.

SEQUENCE 2.

Three robbers burst out of the front doors of the West Brandon Credit Union. One is dragging the branch manager along by the elbow. *Dragger-Thief* gets to a parked car idling at the curb and throws the manager into the back seat. He slides in after his hostage, pushing him toward the other door. The thief with the bag of loot gets in the other side bookending the hostage into the backseat middle. The last thief hops into the front passenger seat and the getaway car peels away.

It picks up speed fast, approaching a vehicle-width bottleneck caused by a double-parked van. In that distance, a sock is pulled off a foot. The bare foot pokes itself out from the front of the van. The foot plants itself firmly onto the asphalt just in time for the getaway car to run right over it.

CRUNCH! The foot glows. The car swerves and crashes into a parked truck up the block and the getaway driver tumbles out. He sits on the ground, caressing his own crushed foot.

Passenger seat thief bursts out of the car, looks across the hood in disbelief. "What the fuck!"

Dragger-Thief leans forward between the front seats and yells at the driver, frantic, "Get back in the goddamn car!"

Fed up, *Passenger-Thief* bolts around the front toward the driver. We're watching him at a distance now, going off on the crippled wheelman as a figure emerges from out between the double-parked van. He hobbles in a *one-shoe-on-one-shoe-off* style toward the crooks.

Driver has passed out from the pain. Passenger-Thief kicks him out of the way, wrenching the door open as far as he can. He can't quite get in however as... *WHACK!* He goes down convulsing. Electrical arcs flash about a gob of plasma on his chest.

Loot-Bag-Thief finally reacts. "Tell me what the fuck is happening man?"

Dragger-Thief just shakes his head. Both jump out of the backseat doors simultaneously, guns drawn. They're gawking all around, ready to shoot anything out of the ordinary.

Dragger's downright panicked. "I don't see anything!"
BIM!

Loot-Bag responds, "Me neither!" He looks to Dragger just in time to see him sliding down the opened backseat door, gob of plasma in the middle of his forehead.

"Shit! Shit! Shit!"
WHOMP!

. . .

ALL THREE ROBBERS AND DRIVER, sit in a circle. Backs are to each other and hands are bound in familiar fashion. They're conscious but too tazed-up to move. Cops are on the scene and one's interviewing the branch manager. Passenger and Driver Side cops are there too. Driver-side cop nudges Passenger Side cop.

"This shit again?"

Man In Suit And Dark Glasses has been eavesdropping on all involved and emerges from the crowd. "You've seen this MO before officers?"

SEQUENCE 3.

Jech crouches on the ledge of a roof in the warehouse district. He puts a finger to a wireless device in his ear. Police scanner is heard through it.

...Repeat possible 071 in progress.

"Kidnapping..." whispers gargoyle Jech.

WRONG! WHAT JECH BARGES IN on is a bunch of drug traffickers. They're cracking open and pouring cocaine out of thousands of those little Pictionary hourglasses. All traffickers focus on him. He realizes what's going on.

"Oh, hi fellas... Lady..." He's trying for nonchalant and failing. *Just level with them idiot.* "Look, I thought I was walking into something... Else. Ok, how 'bout this... I'm quite open-minded when it comes to the substances people put in their bodies... And, as far as free enterprise goes... *Uh...* Let's just say... I'd be the last person to try to bind anyone's invisible hands... I haven't seen anything so disagreeable so I'll just let myself out and you can go ahead and continue realizing Milton Friedman's dream."

Lead trafficker doesn't bat an eye. "Kill him."

"Now you've crossed a line... With me *and* Friedman!"

Five henchmen move in on Jech, reaching for their guns as they go. Jech draws his Glocks and dispatches with them *Josey-Wales* style. *BIM! BIM! BIM! BIM! BIM!*

Meantime, a sixth henchman has snuck up behind. He's rearing back with a pipe. Swings it high and head-wise. Pistols drop as Jech grabs it with both hands. Palms glow. Sting causes henchman to let go. It's Jech's pipe now. He swoops it to the henchman's ankles, toppling him. He punches plasma into his chest.

"Useless," says lead trafficker pointing a TEC-9 faster than Jech can recover his Glocks. He dives behind barrels as trafficker sprays. Bullets barely miss.

Leader barks out at the remaining three lackeys. "What are you waiting for! Unload on him!"

The other three do just that as the leader reloads. The barrels Jech hides behind absorb the bullets for now but if bullet-chews-barrel for much longer he'll be exposed. *PING!* A slug exits two inches from his head. A little pressed-steel flower has bloomed.

He acts on instinct. He picks up a barrel, hugging it. He runs at the gunners. Stray bullets hit him in the arms and legs. Glow.

The gunmen doing the job stop shooting. One collapses on shot-out legs. One nurses a blasted forearm.

Close enough to the two remaining traffickers now, Jech throws the container. Leader ducks, leaving an opening. *WHOMP!* Vigilante takes him out while swooping in on the last shooter currently racking her firearm. He disarms her like nothing but she ain't done. She strikes a fighter's pose. Let's loose.

WHOOSH! WHOOSH! WHOOSH!

He dodges and weaves. She clearly has training but she's only using hand-to-hand on him for the dance, so she can sashay within reach of a discarded firearm. He notices.

"You know what the problem with the black market is?" he asks between defensive maneuvers. "It only ever attracts people already guilty of things far worse than working in the black market." *WEAVE! DODGE! WEAVE!* "If you've highjacked the plane, why not steal the peanuts too? Right?" *DODGE! DODGE! WEAVE!*

He pauses.

She pauses.

He drops the irony. "I'm just some object that's gotten between you and your score, aren't I?"

She sneers. "That's right asshole."

He looks disappointed. He whips out his Colt and... Offers it to her.

She takes it.

She shoots him.

She crumbles.

12

47 SECONDS

Jech's paid the rent. He's sitting in his back booth at The Rio Bravo, marathon runner's 82 on his chest, novelty check beside him, two cordial glasses in front of him. Only a single thing more is required to make this *redux* complete... And it ain't Duckie's cowboy hat.

"Well, well, well."

And there it is. Simmons has once again snuck up on him and he once again wears the expression of pleasant surprise all the way up his sleeve.

"How I feel. How you look. Where we make our wishes. Am I right?"

"Clever."

Bad Joke maybe? "Never mind..." He gestures for Simmons to sit. She does.

"Seems you have some competition," she says unlocking her phone. She slides it to him. As it drifts and spins it's already streaming a news broadcast of Simmons' competition, Bob Cross. He's relating the following news item,

Is the city facing an epidemic of vigilantism? As police continue their search for the man known as 'The Pedestrian'...

Simmons points to Jech and mouths *that's you.* He shakes his head.

...someone else is taking the law into his own hands. This vigilante's weapon of choice: the taser. His nickname: the 'masked flash'.

She grabs the phone back. Turns it off.

"Well?" she asks.

"Just like he says, there's another vigilante out there."

"Except there isn't because that other vigilante is you ya doofus. The witnesses all talk about that yellow glow of yours!" she's grinning at him.

"Stop!"

"Stop?"

"If you want to sit here and drink my beer again you answer my questions this time."

She doesn't even hesitate. "Fine."

Jech's acting like he's won some kind of battle. We'll see... He looks Simmons up and down. He's being intentionally theatrical, like he's really thinking about his pending line of questioning. Then...

"So what's your story? PCP?"

"Ties my shoes in the morning. Next?"

THREE EMPTY PITCHERS. MORE BEER drank this outing than last. Simmons is finishing the anecdote this time. "So that was it. I spun my foot nearly two-thirds the way around my ankle and never danced again. Life's ambition, over."

"I can't imagine. That's so... So disgusting."

"I'm pouring my heart out here!"

"You're too much a bloodhound for your life's ambition to be anything other than reporting."

"Got me," she shrugs. "But I really was a dancer. And I really fucked up my leg."

"And that *really* is disgusting."

"Ha! We're not all indestructible like you Jech." She busts out her best radio announcer voice, "*Able to leap off tall buildings in a single bound!*"

"You're right. I *can* leap off of tall buildings..."

Eyes widen a bit. Is she winning this little game?

"...Because anyone can leap off a tall building. Ya just put your lips together and jump." He mimics a person landing and going splat. His hand features as the person *going* such.

Her eyes narrow back to normal. "You know what I mean."

"Only the mashed flask knows what you mean."

She half smiles. Concern makes up the other half. "I'm not the only person investigating you ya know."

"I know."

"So let me tell your story *Flask*."

"You're not asking the questions remember?"

"I'm not asking a question. I'm making a demand."

"*Touché.*" Now it's Jech's turn to look at Simmons with that sympathy. "Yew're really going to be a dancer."

"A long time ago..."

"I'm not asking a question. I'm making a demand."

She smiles full, unadulterated. She may just be charmed.

He capitalizes. "Busy Friday?"

· · ·

LYTRALL WORKS ON ANOTHER OF his containment units as Jech exits the Black Hole, book under his arm. Digital readout above the door says *10,000 hours*. Jech tosses the book onto the workbench. Title's *Advanced Ballroom Dancing*.

The Professor waves him over to the container.

"About time you learned the ins-and-outs of these microwaves." Wearing welding gloves, he grabs a potato from the workbench. He puts it into the containment unit, shuts the door, hits the button. *DING!* He points to a column of three LEDs. "Ok... *Blue we're cool. Orange ajar. Red released.* Got it?" Jech nods. Prof goes on. "Light is blue, so our potato is not leaving this microwave."

Jech peers closer, examining the spud. "Is it in stasis?"

"No."

SWOOSH!

He takes the tater out of the containment unit and drops it into Jech's hand. Slight glow. "It's lunch." Steam wafts.

"What!" Jech shakes his head. Put's a hand on the container. *Nope. No way man.* Jostles it... "You telling me this thing's an *actual* microwave?"

"Why do you think I've been calling it that this whole time?"

"You put me in a microwave!"

"Only thing that stops you guys..."

A frown. A chuckle. A beat. A laugh. Then...

A realization.

"Speaking of that, what do you think would happen if Dawkitt and I ever actually got into it?"

"Likely The Gimmick cancels out. It would just be two guys fighting. Best man wins and all that." Lytrall appears troubled. Jech notices.

"But?"

"He'll cheat. Be careful."

Lytrall appears no less troubled. Jech is no less aware. "*But?*"

"There's a possibility that... There's a chance... If either of you were to strike a fatal blow to the other the severity *could* cause feedback in equal proportion, then back again, and on. It might enter the two of you into an unending loop of killing each other. Now, you wouldn't actually be killed, you'd be very much alive, but you'd be stuck in that death loop forever."

"Jesus. What are the chances of that?"

"I don't know. Just keep that light blue and we'll never need to find out."

He's again in the passenger seat of Simmons' car. She drives through a rainy West Brandon afternoon, navigating the car through the city as Jech alternates between watching that same city and trying to get his soppy umbrella to close. Windshield wipers slosh back and forth.

She breaks up the monotony, "So what's up? What do you have in store for me?"

"Still want the vigilante's story?"

"Now that his story's a career maker? Nah."

"Funny... One constraint: this is the vigilante's story, not Roger Jech's."

"Understood. I'll refer to you as *The Masked Flash*."

"I hate that name."

"*The Pedestrian?*"

"Hate that one too."

"What should I call you then? Gotta have a name."

"Hang a left here."

She obliges. "Where are we going?"

"To where the story begins."

There's no hesitation in Simmons at all. Either she trusts Jech unabashedly, she's doing what she has to do to get the story, or both. She gives the car a bit more gas. "And what about that name?"

"How about..."

IN THE WORKSHOP JECH SHOWS Simmons some of the tools and toys. Her attention's on the guns.

"So you *don't* use a taser?"

"Sort of. The plasma carries an electrical charge." He picks up the Colt. "Wanna give it a try?"

"Why not? I've always wanted to fire a rifle."

"It's not technically a rifle. There's no rifling in the barrel."

"Does any of that change the fact I've always wanted to fire a rifle?" She smirks. "Relax, that's just the journalist in me."

"Well, with your language games and my nitpicking, there'll be no stopping us."

"...From making everyone puke." Wry turns to simper again, she snatches the Colt. "So what do I do?"

He points to an empty oil canister down the storage facility. "Try to hit that. There'll be a bit of a recoil so put the stock up against your shoulder as hard as you can without tremor."

The stock is off-center to Simmons' shoulder. Jech moves in to correct it realizing he's about to embrace her. He pauses, gestures a *may I* gesture. She bows in assent. He stands behind her, his arms extended and parallel to hers. He corrects her posture and the placement of the stock. They pause for a second mid-embrace... Then...

"Tight on your shoulder. Put the red dot where you want the plasma to go. When you're ready, squeeze the trigger, don't yank."

Bim! Bim! Bim!

The can is struck on the third shot. Not bad.

"Not bad," Jech asserts.

Simmons nods. "Speaking of *not bad*..." She hands over the gun. "When you started out your weapon of choice was standing still. All of a sudden you're *Have Taser Will Travel*?" She looks at him for an explanation.

"That brings us to the last part of the tour." He gestures to The Black Hole.

THEY STAND IN THE SLATE room with yellow grid piping.

"Impressive," she flips.

"Oh yeah? Try shouting out a context. Where have you always wanted to visit?"

"Alright," she says with all due incredulity. Then... "*The Titanic!*"

The slate begins to transform into the requested location. It's the Titanic's grand staircase in all its glory. Woody, brassy, rotund. But... Rusticles appear now, spreading faster and faster all over the walls, covering the stairs and fixtures. A layer of silt amasses on the floors too, climbing higher along the walls. Water's flooding all around Jech and Simmons. It's rushing up to their chests about to be over their heads.

"The Titanic before the iceberg!" Jech shouts, his head tilting backward, water stopping at his lips.

Everything reverts to a dry rusticle-free environment now full of first-class passengers. Jech looks at Simmons with a *that-was-close* expression. "I should have been clearer..."

She's too busy observing things to consider the *mea culpa*. She feels her lapel. "I'm bone dry." She reaches out and depresses the puffy shoulder of one of the passenger's gowns. The passenger is indignant and gives out a haughty *excuse me!* Simmons laughs. "Whoa! You see that?"

Jech's enjoying her enjoying herself. "Everything in here is tangible." He watches her in all her mesmerization for a second, then... "Speaking of *in here*, we can't spend too much time in here." He shouts, "*Time code!*" A digital readout is now superimposed wherever they look in this scenario. It reads,

> *Time Spent in Titanic Rotunda: 2 min. 45 sec...*
> *Time Spent in Titanic Rotunda: 2 min. 46 sec...*
> *Time Spent in Titanic Rotunda: 2 min. 47 sec...*
>
> ...

"There's something I wanted to show you before we go," he insists.

She *hmmms* at him in interest. He hasn't let her down yet...

He shouts, "*Titanic ballroom. Full formal wear.*" The Black Hole transforms accordingly.

She looks down, sees she's in a gown and Jech is in a tuxedo.

He extends a hand to her and affects a formal tone, "*May I have this dance?*"

She attends to all the old-fashioned choreography of the ballroom. Real wistful. She smiles at him. Says in a tone better than appreciative, "You know I can't..."

"You can. If the pressure's too much just put your weight

on me. You'll feel lighter than air." He strikes a dance pose that's only half complete. He needs a partner. "Trust me."

She hesitates at first but since she's facing the most earnest man this side of the Atlantic... She can't help but relent. She embraces him as a dancer would. Music swells and they begin to waltz.

They spin and dip and shimmy and all the rest. Periodically, a slight glow emits from Jech as Simmons uses The Gimmick for leverage. They both operate with expert precision.

Simmons is pleasantly surprised at Jech's ability.

Jech is pleasantly surprised at Jech's ability.

He dips her again then scoops her up. The dance goes on, until...

The choreography begins a slow wavering culmination. But not to a whimper. She spins outward holding onto his hand and he spins her back inward and into his arms. They sashay as he lifts her up by the midsection. He spins with Simmons above him. It is effortless. She's floating.

"Give me a push. Don't worry."

She does. She's propelled into the air, rotating, twirling, basking in the virtuosity of it.

Glow.

He catches her with perfect timing as they embrace. He pulls her close.

The music has stopped but they remain in each other's arms. They're looking deep into each other's eyes and, in what anyone can see coming a mile away, kiss—passion ramping inward and upward.

Unbeknownst to them, the choreography begins again as they, still conjoined, start spinning to the rhythm of a tune that only they can hear.

It goes on until... Abruptly, Simmons pulls away. The

passion hasn't died down any though. Jech tilts his head at her. She smiles a wry smile.

"*Luxury stateroom.*"

The Black Hole begins to transform.

THEY LOWER THEMSELVES TO THE bed of the stateroom, mid-embrace. They begin removing articles of each other's clothing, pausing only to explore and appreciate, inflame and consume of each other. More clothes come off, more foreplay, until... Nude and intwined, they move as though one atop the massive bed.

Simmons rolls over on top of Jech, pinning him down without his resisting. No glow. She's guiding herself downward, hastening the beast of two backs. He stops her, concerned.

"Remember, whatever you do to me, happens to you."

She grins at him, demure, "Then I'm really going to love this." She lowers herself onto him, their pelvises conjoined.

It's in! It's on! It's intercourse! Glow.

Instantly she feels a sensation unlike any she's ever felt in her life. *Ooh.* It's an intensity that defies physiological explanation. It's strange, slightly scary and euphoria-inducing at the same time. It's a tingling elevating pleasure that seems to scream in a language manifesting itself as pure physical arousal, *there's no turning back!* A euphoria demanding she selfishly heedlessly chase the intensifying provocation through to its explosive mysterious but inevitable end. Chase it only for the pursued to double back to pursuer. Nirvana at her heels! About to overtake her? To win out? To win euphoria. A euphoria of amnesia! Fuse is down to the breech!

What Simmons feels is that of a man about to prematurely ejaculate.

Jech's feeling it too. "Slow... Down..."

She thrusts her pelvis onto his, faster. He grits his teeth.

"Wow. Oh wow." She's thrusting faster. Faster still.

"I... can't..."

Jech is supine, Simmons is on top of him, rocking away like a metronome at top speed. That familiar glow begins to swell, beaming majestically from out their crotches. It continues to swell along with Simmons' screams and moans. The glow eventually blots out our entire view with an orgasmic *SWOOSH!*

WHOOOAAAAHHH! HOLY SHIT GODDAMN!

GLOW FINALLY SUBSIDES REVEALING THE stateroom door. The readout above it says,

47 sec.

SHE ROLLS OVER TO HIM, on into his arms. The passion has subsided but the affection hasn't. Neither has the curiosity.

"What the hell was that?" she asks.

He speaks matter-of-factly, "You just had my orgasm."

She stares at him like she's thinking *so that's what happens when that happens!* It's disbelief. "That was incredible... So easy!" She realizes something else about the event... "I need a nap."

She's out cold.

· · ·

THE COUPLE IS OUT OF The Black Hole and back in the hangar. They're collecting their things and putting anything out of place in. Their intimacy boundaries have changed which fits the circumstances. There's a clear disproportionality to the goo-heartedness. Always is. Simmons is casual about it all but for all Jech knows, this is the first relationship for him that didn't begin with his abduction. He doesn't know what rushing it is, what being too aloof is... *Jeez Jech, say something to her, or don't, why not try asking her if she's been on TV again cool guy...* He's got love indigestion. Then...

"Jech?"

"Professor!" He's taken off guard. "Not at your course?"

"My hand." Lytrall holds his hand up with another bloodied rag wrapped around it. He acknowledges Simmons. "Miss."

Jech hops to it. "Uh... Dr. Toll Lytrall, this is Simone Simmons."

"Hi." She bows slightly.

Lytrall reciprocates. "Ms. Simmons." He shakes her hand with his left non-bloodied one. He's very delicate about it. He eyes her discerningly. "You've taken quite an interest in our friend Roger here."

She nods.

"Roger can be quite impetuous Ms. Simmons. Takes a lot of unnecessary risks..." He looks to Jech and his expression softens. He looks back to Simmons, a little softer yet. "...But less and less these days." He tilts his head at the two and squints like he's just hit *Equal* on a calculator and got the sum he wanted. "Well, I'll leave you two alone." He makes for the facility door, stopping at it, turning back. "Pleasure meeting you Ms. Simmons. Off the record of course."

. . .

JECH SITS IN THE PASSENGER seat, again. Outside his apartment, again. He's jangling his house keys *jing-aling-aling.* Not a conscious thought in the world willing him to do it. No room in his head for that.

"What is it?" she asks.

Flood gates. Converts everything at the forefront of his mind to words. Rapid fire. A purging.

"Listen, I know you're a career woman and you have priorities and it's the 21st century and tonight might not have meant for you what it meant for me and I'm just a news source and it's the 21st century and—"

"Roger!" She cuts the engine and snatches his keys. She exits and moves toward the apartment door. He exhales in relief.

She lets herself in.

13

—

CONTEMPORARY SOCIAL ISSUES

We push in on Crimson's containment unit. We push through the green beer bottle glass and on into Crim's abdomen. We're looking at his viscera X-ray style. Inside his stomach, a bottle-fly Tylenol clings. A faint glow emanates from the flesh surrounding the device. An LED starts to flash intermittently.

FLASH ... FLASH ... FLASH ... FLASH.

The device has come online.

"THERE'S THE OBVIOUS QUESTION OF fascism..."

"And what question is that?"

"Well..." the undergrad continues. "The vigilante uses violence as a means to an end. He imposes his will on others, his values."

"All our political leaders do that," Lytrall observes.

The undergrad thinks a second for a rebuttal. A literal second. Resolve. "Yes, but there's a legitimacy in those cases... If not morality. Their actions are sanctioned by the state."

"To be clear," corrects The Professor. "They are *the state* on this use, as *legitimacy* means *law* and the political actors we speak of pass and oversee the enforcement of those laws. But let's focus on a corollary of your claims. Are you suggesting that fascists cease to be fascists once they achieve sufficient political power? Since they would be *the state* in your sense of *state* and of course would sanction themselves?"

A little less resolve... "N—No. No, I didn't mean to imply that. I misspoke. The most well-known heads of fascist regimes all held formal leadership in the nations they ruled."

"So, there must be more to fascism than just violence or imposition of will and values. Otherwise all political bodies would be fascist bodies instead of authoritarian bodies more generally." Lytrall takes out a glass as he speaks. He puts it on the table next to his lectern. The students' eyes widen. He notices. "Relax." He pours some water into the glass and takes a sip. Students chuckle. He continues the dialectic. "I take it by *the question of fascism*, you meant *is The Masked Flash a fascist?*" He carefully enunciates those last few words.

A number of students nod in agreement, emboldening The Professor to explore the matter further.

"Is The Masked Flash... I hate that name by the way... *Ahem*, is The Masked Flash a fascist?" He mouths the words again to himself as though he's going to conquer this tongue twister yet. Then... Focus. "I think the question... I think this particular question..." He sighs. "I think the question *incredibly stupid* quite frankly! And it's not even coming from stupid people, so it's a damn grating one too. Come on guys and gals! Necessary conditions! We discussed this concept for three straight sessions last week. Fascists are collectivists remember? They're violent totalitarian chauvinist types." Lytrall's now making churning motions with his hands. "A distinct political ideology detailing their supremacist attitudes. Everything outside their politic is a threat to their ideal state. They ought dominate every social, political, and economic hierarchy by force *when* not *if* necessary. They detest liberalism, capitalism, individualism, therefore... Come on, you remember this.

"Listen, I know it's all the rage to declare everything under the sun *fascistic*, especially our heroes factual or fictional, but concepts have definitions. Now this tendency isn't exactly new. Pardon the digression: I was in a conversation years ago where a friend of mine had the nerve to suggest that even Batman, of all entities, was some kind of goose-stepping jackboot. I'll say to you what I said to my interlocutor then: get a dictionary. The definitions may not be perfect, definitions never are, yet they lay out some clear necessary conditions *if* never sufficient. And that's all we need to falsify our claim.

"So what do we know? We know fascists are mobbed-up, chauvinist, totalitarian, ideologue, belligerents *by definition*. From what we know of The Masked Flash he works alone. He avoids people by design. He only ever intervenes on those already intervening unjustly in the lives of others. As far as ideology goes, he appears to operate according to just one principle: *put others in harm's way, and I'll be in your way.* He's a live-and-let-live type therefore. Anathema to the totalitarian. But it's the aforementioned principle that's key. The hero only ever intervenes in *second-order*, on those already intervening. A fascist on the other hand intervenes in any order. If no harm is being done and everything is in equilibrium the hero stays home but the fascist goes to work. Unlike the fascist, a peaceful coexistence where all are able to live and let live is the goal of all heroes of recent myth. Is The Masked Flash any different?

"Well..." a student requests rebuttal.

"Go ahead."

"Well, the hero may not meet all the criteria at present, but fascists don't just pop into existence fully formed ready to leap onto tavern tables and stir up ultra-nationalist senti-ment. Surely they have to act covertly at first, ingratiate themselves into larger and larger circles which would require gaining the average person's trust, later dependence. Maybe that's his game?"

"Well posed," Lytrall commends. "Let's keep probing then. What qualities are invariable, or at least *near* invari-able, among fascists-in-the-making? Do we know of any and does The Masked Flash possess such qualities? Keeping in mind that *invariable* is not the same thing as *necessary*?" Lytrall waits. Silence. "Anyone?" He's just about to make this a homework assignment when...

"A lost past," says a student in the back, quiet up to this point. "A past life that was, to him, infinitely better. But a life he believes taken from him. Hitler lamented the loss of a pre-world-war-one Germany for example. Mussolini felt the embracing of liberal democratic values had displaced a more powerful and cohesive Italy, for another."

"Yes. That's it, isn't it. A lost past. Now I hasten to add, don't think that because people desire their future to be more like an idealized time in their past, they're fascists. Near everybody harkens back to a better time from time to time. Their childhood. The days grandma recollects so fondly. Pre-industrial revolution. Pre-modernity. Pre-post-modernity. Pre-*this*-invader-or-*that*. Hell, the majority of people living under fascist rule wished they could go back to a time pre-fascism. You can't very well desire a non-fascist state and a fascist state at the same time can you? If you wish to bring back the past you're almost certainly not a fascist, but if you're a fascist you *will* almost certainly wish to bring back the past..." Lytrall pauses a pregnant pause with these words. His speech goes low and muttered, "So, if The Masked Flash never had a past..." He smiles ever so subtly. "...He'd be alright..."

"What are you saying, professor?" A student up front managed to hear Lytrall's little derivation. "The hero clearly has a past. A history of some sort."

"Of course. Of course you're right. That was just me going off on one of my philosopher's fugues again. Getting caught up in the logic if not reality of the topic at hand. You see, the nature of our reasoning thus far implies that, *if* in some possible world there existed a person without a past, *then*..." The students look like they're trying to maintain interest but intimidation is winning out. Lytrall always loses them with the possible worlds stuff. He decides to let them off the hook. "...Everybody has a past, of course they do. I'm going to leave it to you to further assess the situation and come up with your own answers." He takes another sip of his water. "You've all made very good points. The tough questions are appreciated. Let's end early huh? For next week—" He's caught sight of the clock. "Wow, we're actually *over* time for a change... Alright, next week we start on The Empiricists. Read that passage from Locke I gave you."

14

MILLER TIME

Mentor and Mentee are running diagnostics on Crim's container when... *SQUAWK!* The emergency band of their police scanner barks,

Possible 314 at Old Mill Processors. Possible 314. Officers respond.

"Hostages involved!"
Jech rushes out. Lytrall barely reacts.

IT'S NOT AN ACTUAL MILL. It's an old dog food processing plant, defunct, with tons of overgrowth surrounding it. Jech stalks around the outskirts, moving stealthily, slinking along a utility swath in the outgrowth. A particularly inviting, just recently clipped, utility swath.

He moves gracefully. His thousands of hours of training have allowed for that. But he never trained himself, nor could he, to cheat gravity. He steps onto what turns out to be just a scattering of grass clippings and a creaking sound emits. He stops. Too late...

CREAK. CRACK. CRUNCH!

He tumbles through some rotten 1x6 slats and vanishes into the earth. Gimmick's glow bursts out from the opening of the hole that swallowed him.

He lays impaled at the bottom of what turns out to be a concrete grey water tank. Someone has thrown a set of drag harrows down there. Several of the harrow spikes pierce through his body. Neck, chest, pelvis, right thigh, left forearm, right shoulder. He's pinned in place, still.

In the overgrowth, an armed and heavily geared-up *Soldier-Type* rises to his feet. He looks in the direction of the tank. "He ain't going anywhere," he sneers. He waits a second. "Ya hear me, I said—"

LURGGLELAGELLAGGLE...

Soldier-Type's interrupted by a gurgling rattle. He spins in the direction of it only to see his partner supine. Full of the same holes as Jech. Partner is slightly twitching, just finishing bleeding out.

"Mother fuck!" Soldier-Type crouches in cover. He gets on his walkie immediately. "Target's dead but so's Boggs! He's full of holes!"

A calm voice responds. "Must have set the trap... Keep an eye on the target. And, if you know what's good for you, you'll stay out of its way."

"I repeat: *target is dead!*"

"You have your orders."

Soldier-Type scans the scene carefully. He's dutiful but not stupid. *Something* killed his partner. First thing's first though, he moves up to the tank and looks in... *BIM!* Last thing he expected. "Hell!" He's caught by surprise. He recoils and falls backward.

Jech was waiting for him, Glock in his right hand. He's

aiming it upward though his pinned shoulder won't allow for the appropriate angle.

LYTRALL'S ON HIS LAPTOP CHECKING out the Spread-It sub s/*Masked Flash*. He clicks on a link to closed-circuit camera footage of Jech saving the dog walker.

In the video, we see a long shot going from the roof Jech stands on all the way down to the lot where the attempted mugging took place. Our hero jumps from the roof, flails all the way down and lands face-first. Glow. He then quickly shuffles to get into a crouching position and rises melodramatically. Evidently.

Prof's not pleased. "Damn it! Be. More. Careful."

SQUAWK! "*Motion detected in drive. Motion detected in drive.*" A disembodied voice issues the alert.

"I said be more careful Jech!" He moves to a bank of security monitors. It isn't Jech in the drive. It isn't anyone. He grips his fob, hitting a button repeatedly.

"Won't do any good."

A figure approaches. We can only see him from behind. Figure lets go of several chunks of components previously attached to bottle-fly mechanical men. They hit the floor with a collection of *THUD!*s.

There's a look of recognition on Lytrall's face.

"You."

JECH'S FREED HIMSELF FROM THE harrow spikes. He's propped them up end-on-end and's trying to climb them out the pit. He gets about halfway up and the whole rig gives out, splitting at the center.

CRASH!

Soldier-Type is sitting near the rim of the tank out of taser range. "Whatever you're doing down there stop."

"Wanna know what I'm doing down here? Pop your head in and have a look."

"*Pfft.*"

Jech gives up on the ladder. He lays the harrows against the wall of the tank. Sits on them. He stares up through the opening. "I've seen your type before. Bet there's a guy up there just like you only with air conditioning?"

"Shut up! Don't know how you did him man, but you're dead for it."

"Ah, a friend of yours... Nand didn't tell you that was going to happen did he?"

Soldier doesn't respond right away. Takes us a few seconds to hear his disembodied voice again. Then... "Nand's dead asshole."

Shit. Wonder how he bought it? Jech's affected by this. He's not sad, not surprised, but affected. Curious too. "Nand's moves..." he suggests.

Silence again... Then... "Jane's now."

Jane! Of course. S'what happens when you work with a psycho like that...

He slouches forward on those harrows, raising his palms. He claps his hands until a glow emits. He stares at the tank wall as The Gimmick fades. He claps again. More glow, more illumination. His palms beam outward at us, the glow acting like searchlights.

THE CELL DOOR SWINGS OPEN. Several flashlights shine through the doorway. He's roused by the clatter and light.

Just as his eyes are adjusting to the brightness, *POOSH!* A net surrounds him. He struggles.

We hear Jane's voice. "Pick him up."

Two of Jane's henchmen collect the net surrounding Jech and raise it, raising Jech in the process. He continues to struggle but has no range of motion.

HE'S BOUND TO THAT SAME hand truck, next the apparatus once more. Rat bucket's newly prepped. Jane approaches.

"Where's Nand?" Jech musters. Musters this despite the choke of his fears. He points with his chin at Jane's henchmen. "Who are they?"

Jane doesn't hear this. He doesn't hear it in that narcissistic, Machiavellian, *I absolutely heard you but can't give you the satisfaction of letting you think I'd oblige you in the slightest* kinda way. Instead, Jane's going to try—and fail—to come off as his mentor did. "Looking at the rig again eh? Nand's got it in his head that just showing you this thing will scare you into compliance. You wanna know what I think? I think that until you've actually been underground you don't know what it is to be underground. I think you're just not that scared. Let's change that."

Merc gestures. His henchmen remove Jech's ties to the hand truck though not the ties that bind his body. They inch him toward the hole while he squirms in those bonds.

"I won't run."

Jane's ignoring him again. Gestures to his goons once more. One of them, standing by inert, jumps to action and covers Jech's mouth with a piece of duct tape. Too tight. Glow. The henchman too can't speak. He realizes this and laughs a muffled laugh of understanding.

Jech is lowered into the hole. He can't move his arms. He can't move his legs. He still writhes. From his hips.

Jane's amused at this. "You know you won't die in there don't ya? I bet that's the scariest part."

WE'RE LOOKING AT THE SHALLOW rat-tub of the apparatus. Hand lifts the door flooding it with rodents. Henchmen can be heard carrying on like someone isn't tortured. These rats are a little more bellicose than the previous batch. They fight with each other for the pig gut.

Jech's flipping himself from left to right trying to break his bonds. He fails. There's obvious panic. Muffled screams are heard through his taped mouth.

Jane and his men stand in group, hovering over the pit. It's entertainment for them. A channel tuned to a dog's world. Dog who gagged Jech still can't open his mouth but a muffled laugh is heard through his paralyzed lips. *Muffles* glances over to the rat tub.

A particularly dominant rat has won a grasp of the gut. It clenches the strand in its front paws, sniffing. It bites – *SNAP!* – sending the top portion of the severed viscera shooting upward, through the loop, above and away across the start of the apparatus. The rocks begin to fall *BOOM! BOOM! BOOM! BOOM! BOOM!* ... All the way to the bin. The drop door opens dumping earth onto Jech burying him instantly.

LIKE OF AN ANT FARM...

We're pushing in on a cross-section of the supine Hero. Earth is below him, earth is above him. He can't move. He's as motionless as a corpse. His head is caught slightly tilted.

His chin melded to the top of his sternum. The weight of the earth has pinned him in place. The brightest yellow glow emanates from him though choked by the dirt. There's inaudible, apathetic chatter from Jane et. al. choked the same.

We continue pushing into Jech's glowing body in profile.

We push in and beyond his outside and on to the inside. The sound of the mercenaries fades completely. We can now hear the screams that Jech's grave kept us from hearing out there.

Inside his body we see his internal mechanisms at work. His diaphragm and lungs are moving though, curiously, his heart isn't beating... because there isn't a heart to beat just vacuum. His vocal cords are as active as ever though, generating the most piercing of screams and guttural of groans.

They. Do. Not. Stop.

Above ground we see many active rats but also one struggling to breathe. The dominant rat.

We watch the struggling creature, gasping for air.

Movement lessens more and more.

The rat dies.

HE SHUDDERS, GASPS. SHAKES HIMSELF out of his trance. A pipe above him has been grinding out a churning sound for some time.

He stands. He raises a hand to the opening of the pipe. Liquid hits it. Grey water's started to flow. A sigh. He sighs in relief. "No earth..." Looks up to where he thinks Soldier-Type is. "Forget what I said about *flawless victory fatality* up there. No one who'd work for Jane is capable of friends."

. . .

LYTRALL ASSESSES THE TRESPASSER.

"THOSE mechanical men were expensive… He's not here. Luckily."

"Don't worry. I'm not here for him."

"I meant *luckily* for you."

The figure smirks. The figure is Nand. He's stone-faced as usual but that stone face has been eroded a little. All chewed up. He offers Lytrall what appears to be a telegraph from a nineteenth-century dispatcher. Professor, cautious, reaches for it. Telegraph reads,

Recovery. $7,000,000. $1,000,000 down payment and further instructions at 51.163334, -100.156057.

Head bows. "Should have been more careful… I take it it's Crimson's *further instructions* that brought you here?" He gets defiant with Nand. "You're not taking him without a fight." He prepares for a last stand.

Nand defuses this. "Relax. I'm not here for him either. I'm here for the guy who's here for the guy…"

The power cuts out.

Generator kicks in. Low-intensity fluorescent light illuminates the area.

"They're early."

THERE'S A FRANTIC AIR TO the scene. Lytrall's bapping on the sides of his security monitors. Monitors are dead. He looks to his broken automata at Nand's feet. "Could have used those mechs."

"That was a tactical error," Nand relents.

Professor hammers a big red button on his security console. A red rotating light comes on. "That an apology?"

No time for levity. "Get to your lab," is the soldier's order. "I'm going after Jane."

Grabbing a net gun off the bench, Lytrall heads for the door, stops. "No getting in if you're out." He points to the red rotating bulb.

Nand nods.

THE GREY WATER IS UP to Jech's waist.

He holds his Glock holster and Colt over his head, looks upward in slight concern. "Hey asshole, let this water get any higher and you'll need gills."

"Throw out the guns and I'll turn it off."

"I do that and you'll shoot me… Keep doing what you're doing and I might just let you."

"Fish in a barrel."

"You will be."

"Alright, why ya keep talkin' like you're Master Po or something?"

"Yoda," Jech corrects. Then… "You really have no idea how this works do you?"

LYTRALL RUNS THROUGH THE FARMHOUSE kitchen and bombs down the cellar stairs. *KA-CHUNK-A-CHUNK-A-CHUNK-A.* He stops halfway, runs back up to the kitchen. When he gets there, he grabs a large kitchen knife out of the block on the counter. He turns, and… *KA-CHUNK-A-CHUNK-A-CHUNK-A.*

The lab platform descends. He jumps off before it can land and the platform rises automatically. Puts his knife on the bench to the right then holds his net gun on Crimson's containment unit. Light on the container's blue but everything's pitch black otherwise.

He gropes over his head with his free hand. He finds something up there that satisfies him and gives it a punch. A small generator-powered light comes on. Illumination's barely better than the pitch black. He takes a small digital tablet out of his right pocket allowing for a little more illumination. Readout says,

C. Dawkitt Gen Battery: 99.999%

Approx. Charge: 472 hours.

JECH IS MEDITATIVE. RESOLVE.

"ALRIGHT, I'm throwing 'em up." His Colt flies out of the tank, then the Glocks.

Soldier-Type doesn't hesitate a second, moves in.

RATATATATAT!

He opens up into the water so hastily it's a miracle he didn't shoot his whole clip into the dirt. He looks into the tank, cautious. It's dark. All he can see is what's lit by the tiny flashlight at the end of his M4. Submerged harrows. Then...

SPLOOSH!

Jech bolts up swinging one of those harrows, arcing it up, onto, and *into* Soldier-Type's boot, pinning him to the ground. Soldier-Type struggles to pull his foot free as Jech rears back with his right fist, plasma lightning across his knuckles. He swings, punching into the bottom of the harrow sending the electric plasma flashing all the way up it. Soldier-type convulses, falling forward into the pit with a splash.

"Great," Jech says holding Soldier's head above water. "Now it's a fuckin' party."

· · ·

THREE MERCS HAVE SITUATED THEMSELVES at various points of strategy around the homestead. They stand like basemen on a ball diamond. *Second Base* watching the gate, *First* and *Third* watching home.

Third looks to First. Sees First standing overwatch under a tree. Third looks back to the house. *THUMP!* Third's attention snaps back to First, to the direction of that *THUMP!* He sees First standing overwatch under a tree. Everything's fine. He looks back to the house.

Everything *isn't* fine. A closer look at First Base would have revealed the merc's out cold. Nand's dropped from a tree bow right on top of him and is holding him up by the belt. He's keeping First's head at attention by holding the back of his balaclava in his teeth.

Third base follows protocol. He looks back to Second minding the gait. Second's just doing his job. All's good there. Third looks over to First Base. First's crumpled in a heap.

Third Base is just starting to react as arms come out of the darkness looping around his neck. He's put to sleep.

Back to Second, the last of our basemen still conscious. Second's still just staring down the long gravel driveway. Same fate... *THUMP!* Everything's dark.

THE GREY WATER'S UP TO Jech's neck. We see he's hung Soldier-Type over the rim of the tank waist-up on the ground and ass-down into the pit.

"You better hope I float dummy, or you're gonna drown in that dirt."

Water stops.

"Lucky you."

He listens for who's manipulating the waterworks.

Several sets of footsteps can be heard along with inaudible chatter. The only thing he can make out is, "Jane's not gonna like this."

He submerges himself into the grey water just up to his nostrils. Then...

SMACK! SMASH! CRUNCH! Two of Soldier-Type's colleagues splash into the tank behind him.

He remains still, wary, four-fifths of himself still submerged, when...

A hand thrusts downward into the tank. It's gesturing for him to take it. He notices the slash scar running across the palm. He takes that hand without hesitation. Rises.

He stands face to face with the soldier who saved him back in that bush. Holds up a count with his fingers. *Three.*

Etty nods, suggesting, *saved your ass again. CLAP!* The two connect right hands hard enough to bring out the glow.

Catcher has entered the farmhouse. Catcher is Jane.

He stands bathed in the weak fluorescent light of the kitchen, surveying. He puts what looks like a cigar in his mouth and pops it on. Turns out to be a small flashlight. He holds a simple hand-drawn schematic in his hands, scanning it with the incandescent stogie. He focuses the light on a red circle looped around the back corner of, presumably, a floorplan of the kitchen in which he stands. His head tilts up and turns like on a swivel. Flashlight searches for the object circled.

SQUAWK! Goes a speaker to Jane's left.

Motion detected in-

KABOOM!

Blows the source of the disembodied voice all to hell with his 410. He's fast but dangerous... But edgy too. That voice spooked him and it was more the startle that pulled the trigger than anything else. So, guy's *really* dangerous.

He reloads and holsters the 410 resuming his scan. He stops at the cellar door. Light pops off. He pockets the flashlight and schematic. Makes a first move toward the cellar when...

SWOOSH!

Nand's flanked him, left arm chopping across his chest as the other back-hands his hamstrings. Maneuver flips Jane supine floating. Nand smashes him into the linoleum for his sins.

THUMP!

LYTRALL HEARS THE RUCKUS ABOVE. He fights a desire to examine the source. He could look up and back but he'd be ignoring Crim in the process. Best to just meditate on those blue LEDs.

MEANWHILE, NAND HAS JANE PINNED with a knee to his chest and another to his waist. He takes the 410 off him and lets him up. Holds the 410 on him from the hip.

Nand is stony but his eyes are discerning.

Jane is slightly slack-jawed, tip of tongue protruding, eyes narrow, *blasé blood-lusty*. His slack jaw grins a little. "Lookin' spry for someone with a face full of my bird shot... You should be smelling like a fucked vagina a dog's been shitting out of by now."

"Can't you see my halo Jane?"

POW!

410 fires from the hip blowing a bloody hole in Jane's chest.

"*FUCK! SALT! ... NEVER COULD TRUST ME TO NOT MURDER THE WHOLE WORLD IN ITS SLEEP COULD YA!?*" Jane massages his stinging, superficial wound. "...That's why I had to kill you."

"Sure taking your time with that."

"Well," Second-in-Command grimaces, mocks, "*We don't do, what others do, where doing that gets people dying...* Do we?" He keeps on massaging the salt wound.

Nand holds up the unspent shell of bird shot. A signifying gesture. He holds up the 410 in his other hand, just as significant. He tosses the two objects in opposite directions and moves toward Jane. Time to settle this like warriors.

Jane lunges swinging a right, fast but telegraphed. Nand blocks with his left arm, plunging his right palm into Jane's chest simultaneously winding him and knocking him on his ass. Jane struggles to get up, dropping a fob as he does. Midrise, he lunges again, clumsy.

THUMP! BOOM! BANG! LYTRALL'S ATTENTION is still fixed on the bumps and rumbles above him but his sight is on Crim. He checks that his net gun is ready to fire.

IN THE KITCHEN WE SEE that the fob Jane's dropped is blinking a blue LED. Started at the exact moment...

SWOOSH! LYTRALL TILTS HIS HEAD at the sound, examining the containment unit door. Light is blue. Everything appears as it should. As much as it can appear like *anything* in the dim. Then... The loudest *THUMP!*

Adrenalin and reflex win out, spinning Lytrall one-hundred-eighty degrees to the fight above. What was he thinking? Is he gonna see through two whole floors?

Professor frowns at his haste, begins turning back to his only responsibility. Then... His pivot slows. It doesn't stop, just slows. He puts his finger to the CODA trigger now and picks up speed. Rotates as fast as he can to catch—

The figure's on him!

Lytrall's disarmed before he can even get a third of the way around. The net gun fires off at nothing as Crimson tosses it away across the lab. The pair are now in a face-to-face, fear apparent in The Professor's expression. It's just that though, *appearance*. A bead of blood runs out of his mouth. A glance down reveals Crimson has plunged a large chisel into his gut. Who knows how Crim got it?

We move back up and on Crimson. He's not smirking, not grimacing, just staring. Staring at Lytrall like a toll booth operator handing someone his change. "Blue we're cool," he mocks. Then...

A yellow glow from below. Lytrall's kitchen knife is in his attacker's gut. He's stabbed Crim in the exact place Crim had stabbed him.

The Professor's expression of pain multiplies due The Gimmick but he doesn't take his eyes off his ward. "I had to know," he labors. He twists the kitchen knife. Blood gushes from his own now compounded wound.

The glow in Crim's gut only intensifies but he's not breaking eye contact either. "Well now ya do," he says cold as ice. He reaches down, pulls out both blades as Lytrall slumps over. Crim catches him. "Whoa whoa pappy. I ain't done wi'chu yet." He holds The Professor upright and stomps on the floor. The laser light scans and the lab door begins to descend.

He lowers Lytrall against some cabinets. Blood is everywhere. Crim stays crouched. Wants a look. Looks into the pale mentor, deep... Wants a word too. "Now," he begins. "You're not gonna die right away an' I couldn't be happier 'bout that. See, nothin's gonna bring you back from that ever approachin' abyss but you've still got those precious few minutes to do nothin' 'cept think 'bout me. Think 'bout all I'm gonna do with my freedom. About your failure to stop it... Your failure simplicitor. Your last moments will be your worst for that an' I honestly couldn't be happier 'bout it all."

Lytrall attempts a response but his voice breaks. He lets his expression indicate the content of his thoughts. He betrays the appearance of relief.

Crim's demeanor alters near imperceptibly. He's agitated by this defiance. He reaches down to the floor of the lab and brings his finger back up to The Professor's mouth in a *shoosh* gesture. A shoosh at first. He swoops a frown of blood across the philosopher's lips.

"That's better."

Professor looks to be mustering all the strength he has left. A whisper, "He'll stop you."

It's contemplation for a tick then Crim reverts to the mean. To soulless. "You ramblin' old man. Keep me in your thoughts woncha." He gets on the exit platform and rises out of the lab.

BACK TO NAND AND JANE going round and round. Jane looks beat bad and spent while Nand looks hardly the worse for wear. It's a one-sided fight and Jane knows it. He throws a few wild punches as his boss maneuvers around them putting him in a sleep hold.

"Nighty night."

But...

Abrupt...

Boss releases Jane pushing the dazed usurper across the kitchen toppling him. Push wasn't for nothing. Nand weaves to the left as a kitchen knife comes flying from out the space between his right arm and torso. He grips the attacker's forearm in his right hand, tight, using his left to dislocate attacker's thumb. Knife falls.

Glow.

Nand recoils from the new combatant, sizing him up as he backs away. Something else catches his attention. He glances down. Sees his thumb just flopping there. Looks up. "How'd you get out?" He moves further away setting his thumb back in place with a *CRACK!*

Ears shift. Nostrils flare. He watches the rising-but-unsteady Jane and the empty Crimson a second, then... He welcomes both comers to the fight. Comers move in.

Nand alters his technique for Crim but continues clobbering Jane. He gouges at Jane's lower legs, sweeping him to the floor, then jumps in the air kicking Crim's chest. He puts both boots to Crim like he's using his torso as a launchpad. Crimson flies back into the living room while The Gimmick drives Nand—supine in the air at this point—straight down into Jane at a thousand miles an hour. He's counting on The Gimmick as he has his elbow out and ready.

CRUNCH!

Jane gasps. Nand takes something off him then rolls away.

Crim's back in the kitchen and Nand's on his feet. Villain flashes the kitchen knife in the soldier's direction but soldier reveals what he took off Jane. Ankle and wrist restraints. Crim doesn't react. Nand starts whipping the restraints around like a manriki.

Crim approaches slowly.

Whipping those shackles defensively, Nand tries to get a read on his opponent. No telegraphing from Crim. No *anything.* He switches from defense to offense. He whips the shackles left to right, right to left; left left; right right; then in no discernible pattern. He increases the speed with which he spins and whips those shackles.

It works. Crim's distracted for just a millisecond. Nand makes a move in less than that millisecond. He swings the restraints at Crim's right forearm. Chain loops around arm three times fast. He catches the cuffs on the last go-round, locking them onto Crim's wrists, finishes the job by latching the feet restraints to the oven door and refrigerator.

He backs away from his opponent now slashing slashes cut short by the shackles.

SMACK!

Jane's sucker punched him in the right of his jaw, stumbling him. He shakes off the daze. "Forgot about you."

Traitor just wheezes hard at him and pants harder. He stands cradling his left ribs in his right arm.

Before either combatant can make any other move, a hissing swells. Crim's broken open the propane line that feeds into the top of the oven. He's readied the kitchen knife, looking for something to make a spark. Stove outlet's in reach. He places the tip of the blade into the hot slot and prepares to drive it home.

Jane and Nand aren't finished but they are done. Thanks to Crim they don't have a choice. They split in opposite directions and bolt for the exits closest them.

Tip of the knife smashes into the outlet.

.   .   .

WE'RE LOOKING AT THE FARMHOUSE front on, when... Nand and Jane burst out opposing windows simultaneously. Nand bursts out the kitchen window left of the house and Jane bursts out the living room window to the right, just before...
     KABOOM!

15

THE MENTOR

The panel descends in choppy increments. Nand has propped one end of a 4x4 up against the cellar ceiling and the other on the toe of a jack-all. With each wrench on the jack lever the lab entrance lowers a few inches.

Gets it open just enough to squeeze through. He rolls into the lab.

Lytrall sits in a heap, blood pooled around him, coagulated. He's not moving.

"Oh no." Nand crouches down, looking over the wounds. Looking dire.

A weak but insistent whisper issues to him, "You should go."

Proof of life snaps Nand into *Action-Nand*, like he lives for cold effectiveness and not this lamentation bullshit. "How do I release that platform?"

Weaker yet, "Stomp three times."

Nand stomps. Scan. Platform begins to descend.

"All right professor, let's go."

"No point trying to save me..."

"Your dying's not going to be a result of my choices." He puts pressure on Lytrall's wound while scooping him up at the same time. They move toward the exit.

Groaning, "You're starting to bother me…"

NAND BURSTS THROUGH THE ER doors, Lytrall in arms, barking orders. "Got a severe abdominal puncture! Gonna need a transfusion and a vascular surgeon!"

Nurses and health care aids pour out of nursing stations and triage. Professor is quickly eased onto a stretcher. Pressure is put on his wounds as he's wheeled away out of Nand's sight.

Doctors and nurses have swarmed the stretcher. They're so frenetic everything is a blur. Chaos. The only constant is the bright, nearly blinding lights overhead.

In all this, Nand's disappeared.

"Prep an op theater and get his blood type!" a doctor shouts.

Lytrall spits blood and coughs. He struggles against the weight put on his abdomen to control any bleeding, wincing in a pain proportional to the increasing pressure. Maybe he's not so wrong to protest? The horror and trauma he's faced can't have left much blood to contain. His pallor corroborates this… Then he writhes, arms outstretched. Staff not working on him try to hold him steady. Abruptly, his waving right hand stops and clenches into a fist. He slowly raises it perpendicular to his torso.

Medical staff work around it.

He glances up to the clenched hand that did the damage. A small bead of blood runs out from the creases his index finger makes due the clenching. The running of the bead changes direction as he rotates his fist to get a better look. A single drop of blood falls in slow motion. The Professor's visage follows the bead from fist to now motionless chest.

At the point the droplet ever so slightly spatters to rest, his face is completely still, eyes open and fixed. His arm now by his side.

"He's in arrest! No pulse!"

Someone in all the chaos begins chest compressions. He's still motionless, eyes fixed. They don't pound on his chest. They don't get out the defibrillator and shout *clear!* That doesn't work when there's zero cardiac activity. They just perform a few more compressions then stop, every one of them looking like they wish there was a reason to continue but also like they know death when they see it.

IT'S ALL JUST THEATER. JECH follows Etty down one of the many boulevards of Old West Brandon. Rebel stops at the ticket counter of a revival theater, gesturing that *this is the place.*

Jech's confused. Etty ignores this and shimmies up to the top of the box office. He disappears for a second, then drops behind the box office glass, then disappears again. The front doors of the theater open and he ushers Jech in.

There are old movie posters everywhere, lots of burgundy curtains and plush carpeting. There are also two cots in the corner of the lobby, a hot plate, water thermos, food containers, and not much more.

"Home sweet home?" Jech suggests.

Etty pats him on the shoulder, smiles, then holds up a *wait just one second* finger. He goes into an office behind the concession counter.

Jech stays in the lobby, moving along the row of old

posters waiting for the rebel to finish rummaging. He recognizes some posters, others he doesn't. He leans in for closer looks at those he does recognize. As he peruses, the French doors at the theater's entrance open.

Hand goes to bottle-fly Glock. He spins to the entrance. Nand enters.

Jech's face suggests calm though his chest has begun heaving. Gun's gripped tight though still in holster.

Nand looks like he's been expecting him. "Jech, I—"

But vigilante's already rushing the soldier, bridging the gap like teleporting. He's using hand-to-hand before those hands are even in reach—glock in one of them.

Art's proficient if not effective. Nand dodges Jech's flurry easily, disarming him the same way he disarmed Crimson. He pops his redislocated thumb back in place.

Jech keeps on. *UPPERCUT!/DODGE. ELBOW!/DODGE. GRAPPLE!/BREAK.* Then... the two separate. Square off.

"You were supposed to tell him!" Nand shouts in all directions. Focus returns to Jech. He tries for calm. "Listen to me boy..."

He makes the mistake of searching for Etty for just a second and Jech capitalizes. He draws his remaining pistol in left hand and shoots Nand with extreme prejudice. *BIM! BIM! BIM!* Two to the chest and one right between the eyes. Nand collapses.

The Interventionist moves toward his quarry, pounding floor as he strides. Not fast, not slow, just with some sort of bursting animus that distorts time. Nand's staring up at him, barely, watching what of him he can, not happy to be defenseless. Soldier's only able to move his neck at present but that doesn't stop him from using it to the full extent that he can, like he's trying to lift a watermelon with a flyswatter.

Is Jech gonna pounce? Something else? We'll never

know because just as the gap between he and Nand is about to vanish, Etty slides in and wedges it closed for all involved. *No-no* he gestures. Jech keeps pushing like little Etty isn't even there. Rebel changes tack. He puts his scarred hand up to his throat and slashes a finger across it.

Jech stops. *This better be good ol' buddy.*

Etty holds up a felt pen and lures Jech away. They move toward some posters and stop at *The Magnificent Seven*. The one with the large '7' running top to bottom, Eli Wallach in the center, McQueen and Brynner at the top. Etty motions for Jech to pay attention. Jech obliges the rebel but half keeps an eye on Nand. Etty's circling the farmers' village on the poster. He points to the village then himself. Village, himself.

Jech comprehends. "You... Your people."

Etty nods. He circles Eli Wallach.

Jech anticipates. "Nand."

No no! The rebel admonishes with a shake of his head. He draws a standing stick figure next to Eli. He points to the stick figure then to Jech, *that's you*. He then draws six supine stick figures, clockwise, around the Jech figure, in symmetry, and lastly an arrow from Eli to the supine figures.

Jech gets it. Looks surprised. "Bandits? Bandits attacking your people?"

Close enough Etty shrugs. Now he circles Yul and slowly points a finger. The finger stops at a still mute though attentive Nand. Jech's incredulous, angry even.

"Bull-fuckin'-shit Etty! And let me guess..." He grabs the felt pen and circles Steve, then writes above the circle, *Jane*.

No-no, shakes Etty. He takes the pen back and frantically scribbles out 'Jane'. He starts at the 'E' and scribbles all the way to the 'A', too hasty to erase the 'J'. He waves an *over here* gesture and hustles to a *Commando* poster. He grabs a

Pringles container on the way, opening the top and dumping the chips out. He points to the poster then jams the bottom of the Pringles container up against his chest like it's gone right through him. He holds the container with one hand and does his best Vernon Wells impression. He smokes the felt pen like a cigarette with the other, alternating between exaggerating the smoking and exaggerating the chest wound.

Jech points a finger to the writhing, smoking, Etty. "Jane?"

Etty nods vigorously. He opens his arms and slightly embraces Jech at the shoulders. *You got it!*

Jech shakes his head. "I can believe Jane betrayed Nand because *I know* Jane is Bennet enough to do it. But pardon my incredulity at the idea that Nand was in that bush to help you."

"It's true." Nand is up on one knee, wobbly. He looks sore, sore like a person who's been exploded, electrocuted, and had his thumb dislocated twice. "That's what Etty's Premiere was payin' us for. Only it weren't bandits attacking his people. They were Legault subsidized paramilitary—"

Jech ain't hearing this just yet. "None of that changes what your lapdog did to me in that earth." He's back in attack mode, but...

"Stop boy." Nand's put a hand up. "He fooled us all. Rip my head off for negligence next week." He tosses something to Jech. "Right now you need to listen."

It's Lytrall's all-purpose fob. There's a smear of blood on it. Jech Comprehends.

HE MOVES TOWARD AN ER nurse at her station.

"Toll Lytrall?"

The nurse stands, taking Jech by the arm and shoulder as she rises. "Please, sit with me..." She leads him to some waiting room chairs to prepare him. "I'm sorry. He died a little over an hour ago."

His eyes glaze. Slight glow. He slumps into one of those chairs.

"Are you family?" the nurse asks.

He appears to be on the verge of something. His glazed eyes well up now, demeanor is silent and calm otherwise.

"Sir?"

Still silent...

INSIDE THE MAJOR TRAUMA WARD he stands next to the body of Lytrall, looking at him a last time. Body appears ashen and cold, but at peace. He backs away and the nurse draws the curtain around Lytrall's bed.

"I'm sorry."

HE AND THE NURSE EXIT Major Trauma and separate from each other. He shuffles, moving blankly forward. A man in a physician's coat is approaching him from behind, in a rush, trying to catch up to him at the ER door.

"Mr. Jech? Are you Roger Jech?"

Jech turns.

"I was the attending doctor when your friend was brought in," *Physician-Coat* says this a bit winded. "Seconds before he passed, he said something to me. It was difficult for him to speak, but I believe he wanted me to tell you, *The Gimmick cancels out.* He just kept repeating, *tell Jech The Gimmick cancels out...* I'm sure that's what he said, it was all he could do to even whisper. Does that make any sense?"

"Sort of, yes." Jech notices the doc's expression, like he wants to know more about the arcane statement. "It's a long story... It... It doesn't matter." He looks back to where he last saw The Professor. "What's going to happen to Toll?"

"He'll be taken to the morgue shortly."

"No, I mean, what about a funeral? Final resting place?"

"That's up to the family."

"He didn't have anybody."

"Then I guess that's up to you Mr. Jech."

He nods, his grief worsened by these facts.

Physician-Coat can't help but empathize. "If it makes you feel any better, it isn't your friend in that morgue. Your friend is right here. He's right here with you." He points to Jech's heart.

Jech's noncommittal. He may appreciate these words later if he can shake the triteness off 'em. And, maybe he will. Maybe he *should*. It's a funny thing what happens when we make the slightest effort to hear a platitude as though said for the first time. Pure profundity. These expressions stand the test of time for a reason *doncha know*... Pearls hiding in performative utterance, just begging to be, of all things, *understood*. To be treated as meaningful not functional. *Meaning as use!* Like buying a book of poetry to swat a fly. Oh, but what meaning you would find if you could only hear these words a first time! Maybe someday, but not right now...

He nods at Physician-Coat and makes for the exit. He moves through the hospital doors as grief dominates stride but memory dominates grief. He stops, grasping the rail that leads back to the automatic doors.

"Are you ok Mr. Jech?" The ward nurse has been monitoring him. She issues her concern through the doorway.

He waves her away in that manner suggesting, *thank you, I'm fine*. He just needs a minute.

HE'S TRAINING. SELECTING A BLACK Hole scenario for honing skills of situational awareness.

"Random survival scheme. Max vulnerability," he shouts to the AI. The scene transforms into the mercenaries' camp. Jech's in the pit. Nand's contraption hovers above him. He realizes the implications immediately.

"Oh sh..."

The ton of dirt comes crashing down. He's buried, brought to a kneeling position and confined to it, encased. He can't speak so obviously he can't turn off the simulation.

We're on his screaming viscera again and moving out from the internal screams to reveal the glowing exterior of our sudden captive, silenced, still kneeling, motionless, when... Two hands dig frantically down to his shoulders.

Hands find their grasp and the captive's pulled up and out of the pit.

Teary-eyed and trauma-ridden, he stares at his savior, stares at the man crouching next to him. He stares on the verge of catatonia. The Professor puts a hand on his shoulder. He looks him in the eyes with a brand of sympathy all too familiar. One that a more conceited Jech might think was reserved just for him. The more conceited Jech would be correct in this assumption.

"It's ok," says the mentor. "You have people in this world now Roger. No longer alone." He puts his other hand on the other shoulder. "Let go of the fear... Let go, and a trust will take its place." The mentor stands him up, patting off the dirt. "We may not be able to save the *life* of Roger Jech, dear friend, but we will always be there to save *you*... Always."

Jech begins to crumble. He puts his hand on Lytrall's, looking back at him. He nods. Other hand reaches to his pocket. He takes out the small bottle-fly tablet and gives it back.

HE STANDS AT THE DOOR—A door he's praying will be the last he walks through tonight. It's opened by Simmons. She's pleased to see him but his current state is cause for concern.

"Roger?"

He stumbles through the threshold, not saying a thing. She strokes his cheek with her right hand. He looks at her, face bunching up and twisting. He's happy to see her but still buried in his grief.

"What is it?"

He walks past, not callously, more zombielike, to the couch in her living room. She follows. He sits. She sits next to him. He scootches his seat away from her, then lays sideways putting his head into her lap. Reflexively, she resumes stroking his cheek.

He finally lets those tears fall. Cries, honest to goodness. He closes his eyes on them and they pour. Tight.

16

THREE HOPS

The sign at the gate reads *Fort Bartlett* but the decoding screams: *location of the Federal Security Agency of Amerika East.*

Crimson stands at the northwest entrance of the compound, in a parking lot about thirty yards from the gate. A tin canister of gasoline drops to his right. The wobble and hollow *THUNK* made on landing suggest the canister empty. He zips a raincoat over a collection of mylar bags hanging off his chest. Moves out from between a couple of identical Chevy Malibus. Heads for the security checkpoint.

Guards see him at about twenty yards out. See him in all his cold presumption. Impossible not to. *First-Guard* mans the gate enclosure while *Second-Guard* exits to confront the anomaly.

"Sir, you're not permitted to enter here," Second says, courteous but firm. "Pedestrians must use the south entrance."

Crim keeps walking, puts a hand in his pocket. Second reaches for his sidearm, hand hovering, holster unbuttoned.

First does the same but only after pushing a large button inside the booth.

"Sir!"

Still coming. Crim removes his hand from that pocket. A pistol! Second-Guard pulls his sidearm from its holster. Crim raises his weapon but before he can shoot...

PSSSEW!

A .30-06 round rips through his head exploding it in a downward forty-five-degree beam of yellow. The *KA-RACK!* sound follows. Crim stops, peers into the distance. Peers through his glow, head still cocked at forty-five degrees. Off in that distance the sniper that took the shot falls from a sentry tower.

Glow subsides and he's moving again. Second-Guard and First act carefully at this, perplexed, guns drawn and raised nonetheless. Crim just pounds pavement toward them. They do as trained. *POP! POP!* Two yellow beams shine from out our trespasser's forehead the exact moment the guards' heads burst. Crimson walks on past the bodies.

JECH SWINGS THE MASSIVE SLIDING door of the facility. Inside, everything's trashed. Black hole is rubble. A pile of shiny obsidian chunks. Five heads of The Professor's mechanical men sit in a row, propped up on crowbars as though heads on stakes.

"Not sure whose counterpart did this. Yours or mine." Nand stands behind Jech in the entryway, Etty's to his left.

Not in the mood for small talk, Jech sifts in silence. There's a flickering and flashing coming from the rubble to his left. He digs out the source. A chunk of marble containing the digital readout. It flashes *8,760,000:00*.

"A thousand years," he says.

"What does that mean?" Nand asks. He's snuck up over Jech's shoulder and is trying to make sense of things.

Jech backs up into Nand taking the soldier away with him. *Back up outta my business old man.* He then turns, answers him but as if speaking more for a world unaware. "Imagine a man with a hundred lifetimes' worth of your training. If nurture beats nature, we're shit-under-shoe cuz our man just experienced a millennium of *nurture* in the time it takes to walk through a door." He rubs at his face. Looks exasperated.

Etty watches this with concern. Nand watches with annoyance.

Jech looks up. Looks up at nothing. Looks up like he's looking at nothing, like he's got nothing left. Because...

Defeatism so easily follows alarmism, doesn't it? It's the design.

Your situation is dire you see, you're right about that. In fact, it's worse than you could ever imagine. And it's true, there's nothing you or anyone like you can do to remedy it. Only I can help you, but you must first put your fate in my hands and my hands alone, completely, where this means hastening a world you've never known and couldn't possibly understand... But need. Know too that everything I do from here I do for your good and your good alone, no matter what is done or what results. I work in mysterious ways. I see you're already prepared to let me save you, child. Now it's your job to ensure the others are prepared too...

It's a recipe for monsters to do what they do: suit themselves in a world that must first give permission.

He continues the lament, "I can't beat him... Not without—"

"Stop whining about that pathetic old man," Nand barks.

"W—What'd you say?"

"I said, if that old man had been more careful he wouldn't have let Crimson get the drop on him and he wouldn't be on that slab. He's pathetic."

Etty watches the pair discerningly now, paying special attention to Jech's eyes. Eyes flash rage. What's about to happ...

Vigilante lunges!

Nand steps out of the way letting his attacker stumble right on past. Shakes his head in disappointment... "Boy, you fight like every one of your opponents can't fight back because they can't. For that, you telegraph everything. Crimson telegraphs nothing. There's nothing behind those eyes." Soldier tenses. He and Jech begin to circle each other. Fighter's stances engaged. "But I got the upper hand on him. Once." It's Nand's calculus now, "By transitivity, if you can get the upper hand on me, you can get the upper hand on him."

Nand nods. Etty nods enthusiastically.

Jech comprehends.

Fine.

He lunges once more. *WIFF! WIFF! WIFF!...* Nand dodges everything.

"We default to letting our emotions lead. Put a switch in that hardwiring and set it to *off.*"

Sanctimoniousness and hesitancy are baked into the haphazard performance now. "I'm not like the men you train. I'm no callous monster." *WIFF! WIFF!*

"Neither were my men. Be a sentimentalist around grandma. Be an intuitionist around your enemies. Don't think. Don't feel. Just move."

He's pensive. He strikes. Nand dodges.

"Don't think."

He's irritated. He growls through his next attack. Nand Dodges.

"Don't feel."

Exhales. He attempts a calm. He pulls it off?

"Move!"

He bursts out into a flurry of lefts and rights. One actually connects. *CRACK!* He looks to the soldier, half for approval half wondering how bad he hurt him.

Nand reaches out slapping him on the forehead. Li'l glow. "Pathetic. Jane was right to put you underground. His only mistake was digging you out."

Progress reverts so easily to one. Jech's angry and punching wildly again. Nand's dodging everything again.

"Be two things at once boy. Dampen what of the two isn't needed, amplify what is." Soldier makes himself vulnerable to attack. A real invitation. "Now tear me to pieces!"

Jech attempts calm again, eyes close. He gives himself a beat. Another... One more... And... *He's right Jech. Hate him for getting to this knowledge before you. Hate him for sharing it so graciously. But keep him from it, for when he sees it in you he sees all of you.* Eyes open to reveal the face of the nemesis...

Nand can almost swear those eyes have turned an ashen grey... A dead grey. Inside that grey there might just be nothing but the grey's so uninviting who would want to see behind to confirm?

BOOM! Left hook outta nowhere catches Nand's jaw. Now Jech let's go with a right hook. *BOOM!* Other side of Nand's jaw.

Soldier tries to shake off the daze... Can't.

Now's the time for that flurry. Like a blur Jech's rights and lefts pummel Nand's ribs. *RIGHT/LEFT, RIGHT/LEFT, RIGHT/LEFT* ... Images of The Merc of a previous life fraternizing with the eternally wretched Jane intrude upon mind's eye ... Forces the flurry for a good five seconds more, *RIGHT/LEFT, RIGHT/LEFT, RIGHT/LEFT* ... Then, seamless to the action, he hoofs Nand in the midsection full force. Sends him sliding ass-to-ground across the floor.

Looks like there should be cartoon cuckoo birds chirping around Nand's head. Barely able to sit upright anyway, he gives in and falls backward.

Jech stands triumphant, eyes glowing with humanity again.

CRIMSON STANDS IN A DESERTED parade ground. Deserted save for a few dead guards about the place. Some wet is evident on his coat. His attention's on the shiny black FSA building over the horizon, his quarry.

He's going to bat that mouse around a little before he eats it.

QRF soldiers burst onto the scene armed and armored, teeth-to-toes. They surround Crimson. He's motionless a moment more. Assessing a moment more. Then... He whips out that damned pistol of his.

They open fire on him only mowing themselves down in the process. Invisible bullets chew the shit out of 'em. The more accurate infantrymen kill themselves instantly while weaker shooters see their necks burst in bloody puncture, lungs pop, even kneecaps explode. The mylar bags burst all over Crimson as beams of yellow pierce from where the fluid pours. It looks like all the midday sunshine in the world is trying to escape Crim's body one bullet hole at a time.

Someone's fumbling with a hand grenade trying to ready it. Crim catches this. Moves toward *Fumble-Soldier* effortlessly closing the gap. Pin's already pulled but

Fumbler's still holding the safety spoon. He's at a loss for what to do next. Crimson puts out a hand and gestures for the grenade, makes an *it's alright, you can give it to me* face. Confused, the soldier obliges. Safety spoon pops off and he drops the grenade in the waiting palm. Crim holds the grenade in both hands, up to his chest, like a treasured possession's just been returned.

He turns and walks off.

BOOM!

A fragmented glow like a thousand pincers of groping light reaches out the front of Crimson. Simultaneous to the burst, the soldier who gifted the grenade blows into several pieces in several directions matching the pincers. Head's ripped off. He loses an arm. Torso detaches at the waist save for a flap of skin at the bottom right. Torso swings from right hip like on a hinge.

At this point, surviving infantrymen have caught on to the suicide that is blasting at Crim. They move in *en masse*, using hand-to-hand.

Crim stands still. Why waste the energy? All attack him with proficiency which only causes the men to send themselves flailing. Looks like a rugby scrum launching human beings out of it.

Enough brawlers have fallen to allow Crimson a use of his own skills. *CRACK! CRACK! WHOMP!* Soldiers still fly but not of their own doing. Crim's blows see to that. A few others who can block effectively only ensure their hands turn to mush as Crim happily breaks his own on their armor. Glow pours out of his knuckles as blood pours out of theirs'.

Crim keeps on. Fights like Jech but faster and more vicious, preferring body blows to holds or legwork.

A particularly adept combatant squares off with him.

Combatant knows to just dodge never block or attack. Crim adjusts, moving so fast no one can see a thing. *LEFT/RIGHT, LEFT/RIGHT...* Can't call em *hooks* can't call em *uppers*. They're more like gouges maybe? If you said Crim was tearing pieces of this guy's guts out and putting them back at-once you'd have a far more accurate account.

LEFT/RIGHT, LEFT/RIGHT... Opponent collapses, viscera shredded for tripe as another soldier gets the drop on Crim from behind. Puts him in a sleeper hold. Glow. Soldier's dazed quick. Falls away, unsteady. Crim backs up wearing Sleeper-Soldier's grenade pins on fingers.

BOOM!

Sleepy explodes taking a few others with him.

Three brawlers remain. Crimson strikes a pugilist pose. Low and loopy. He takes a few swings at the trio, overextends himself and trips due his own momentum. The second he's on the ground the men commence stomping on his face like they're putting out a fire. Two of the three just knock themselves out suggesting to the third that he really needs to put his back into it. Third leaps into the air and stomps with tremendous force. His face hollows the second his foot makes contact. Blood shoots out the ears of his now concave head.

Then...

POOOSH!

Crimson's netted. He thrashes.

POOOSH!

He's netted again.

POOOSH! A third time.

Still stands. Still thrashes.

An MP rushes over with a taser wand. Moves it toward Crim real impetuous. Before he can make any contact, the arcing tip ignites the gasoline of those mylar bags.

WAH-HOOF!

Crim's ablaze like a whicker man telic. He burns away calm, just watching the MP who lit him up. There's a patience in the observing that all present can't help but notice a second. Then... MP begins to smolder. No flames but his hair's melting. He screams, tries removing articles of clothing. His skin is sizzling, blistering, boiling. Screams louder...

Other soldiers look on in disbelief. How can they stop this? What is it they'd stop?

MP's skin is sloughing off in chunks. He's charring more and more. He topples.

Body's burnt to a crisp inside a pristine uniform.

In all the horror the men have lost track of Crim. He's gone but not to flame. No charred corpse only smoldering nets. Last remaining flames flicker...

THE WATER HITS NAND'S FACE with a *SPLASH!* He stirs. Jech and Etty reach out to lift him. They hold him upright as he collects himself.

"Ugh shit," he groans. "You might actually stand a chance."

Jech's indifferent just yet. "This would still be a hell of a lot easier with The Professor around."

Nand relents. "I know boy. I know."

"At least The Gimmick cancels out."

An optimistic Etty extends both arms and pats the pair on their shoulders suggesting *everything is fine and we're all friends now*. Rebel beams at the two. His Beaming goes unrequited.

Nand's got a point to drive home. "Just remember," his recapitulation begins, "*Two things at once, one thing at a time.*

You're not the opposite of Crimson because of what you *aren't*. You're the opposite of Crimson because of what you *are*."

CRIMSON'S NAKED NOW, COVERED IN soot, surrounded in perfect symmetry by dead warriors. Something wavers in his right hand. He starts out walking for FSA headquarters. Final stretch. Leaves little charcoal footprints in the grass as he goes.

Then...

Three Apache helicopters rise up around him from off the horizon. We all know what's going to happen but we're going to watch it happen anyway. Helicopter Commander gets on the loudspeaker.

"Don't move! You have nowhere to go. We have the area surrounded."

True to form, Crimson isn't backing down. He reveals the object in his right hand. That fucking pistol of his. He ambles backward toward the FSA building, suggesting *try an' stop me.*

Helicopter Commander has no choice. She orders her gunner to fire. A chain gun mounted at the front of the Apache lets loose with a stream of M788 rounds. Gun pumps munition to an allegro *Peter-Piper-Picked-A-Peck-of-Pickled-Pepper* rhythm as bullets strafe across Crim left to right. Three pelt him in the chest as gunner's blood erupts all over the copter's windshield.

Commander takes control of the weapons trying to get a look through the jam. She and the other two gunners open fire. All chain guns find their target as gimmick shreds Commander and remaining gunners. Commander's pilotless copter goes into a spin and smashes into the dirt clockwise, nose to tail, crunching like a beer can.

Remaining two Apaches get into a close formation. Low to the ground and side by side. Apache to Crim's right fires a Hellfire Blast-Frag. Direct hit! Crim glows. Pilot explodes. Naturally, dead pilot's copter goes into a spin. It clips the tail rotor of the other Apache as it crashes. Clipped Apache can't stabilize. Last surviving pilot's gotta eject. *SHOOM!* The blades of his main rotor fly off in multiple directions as he bursts out of the cockpit into the air.

One of the rotor blades spins toward a Crim almost welcoming it. The blade crisscrosses right through his midsection leaving him brandishing a yellow glowing belt. A pair of legs fall to the ground in front of him as pilot's dripping torso parachutes off over the horizon.

PEOPLE SCRAMBLE FOR THE EXIT as Crimson enters the FSA complex. Alarm sounds blare but there's no one of authority left to tell anyone what to do. A slight *Nebbishy-Type* runs along with the herd when he's snatched out from it. Crimson holds him by the collar, tight.

"You come across as sum'un knows how all this works." He flips the nebbish's lanyard into view. What catches his eye are the words *Systems Administrator*. He looks back at the spooked tech. "Systems administrator man, won't you be my Edward Snowden?"

17

MENTOR MENTOR

The old screening room of the heroes' headquarters is a bygone wonder. Everything but the silver screen is a burnished bronze or a plush burgundy. From the chandelier to the faux palace windows flanking the proscenium. From curtains to cushions. You're a fop if you love it and you're a fop if ya don't because ya do... It's comforting to think there was once a time where a ma, a pa, and the kids could sit for an evening in front of the silver of that golden room. The Big Screen. Cartoons for the little ones, newsreels for the big ones, adventure serials for all. And then the A movie and the B movie of that wonderful evening of wonderful golden age entertainment. Wondrous! Jech, Etty, and Nand stand around the proscenium of the theater watching a television that sits on it.

It's a news report. It's Bob Cross droning on,

Although details remain sparse regarding today's siege, Channel Five has confirmed several fatalities, mostly military, although a number of technologists including a systems administrator are among the-

Jech throws the TV remote in frustration. Effort causes the channel to change to religious programming. This time it's an evangelist droning on. Albeit, with less religious fervor than Bob Cross...

As the lord says: "Of the tree of knowledge of good and evil you shall not eat, for in the day that you eat of it you shall surely die."

The evangelizing appears to have struck a chord with Nand.

Jech too, but in a different way. "This is just what we need..." He hits the power button on the TV. He goes off looking for the remote.

Etty eats some condensed soup right out of the can.

Nand remains contemplative. "Jech, you said The Gimmick cancels out," a hint of suggestiveness in this. "How do you know?"

"It was The Professor's last words."

"How did *he* know?"

"I don't know. He was a wise man. He just knew things."

"Think about it Jech. If you and Crimson are the only two of your kind, then how could *anyone* know The Gimmick cancels out? The two of you have never breathed the same air let alone thrown a punch at each other."

Jech's getting a little irritated. "He's no liar if that's what you're getting at."

"That's *not* what I'm getting at. Think about it."

He thinks. Thinks a little more... He gets to where Nand had been getting at. Epiphany? It's something...

He bolts down the aisle, moving to the door. He stops a second, turns to the soldier and the rebel, "He's all alone in there!"

He's gone.

HE BURSTS THROUGH THE DOORS of the ER, second night in a row. He approaches the nursing station, frantic.

"I was here last night..."

"Yes, I remember," says the nurse standing up in her station chair.

"You have to let me see him."

Nurse is hesitant, "I... I don't know that that's possible..."

"Please!"

Another voice, "Mr. Jech..."

Nurse sits back into her chair, lets the approaching authority take over.

"...Maybe I can help you?" The voice belongs to the man in the physician's coat, though he's *sans* coat. Must have gotten off shift. He sits himself in one of the waiting room chairs gesturing for Jech to join him. Jech does. Physician-Coat looks sympathetic but also like he's making a diagnosis. "What's on your mind Mr. Jech?"

"I need to see Dr. Lytrall." He's shaking a little.

No mincing words, "I'm Sorry. He's been cremated."

"Impossible! I need to see him!"

"I'm sure they can arrange to have his remains released to you, you being the closest to family he had, so you can have him interned."

Slight pleading, "I need to see him."

Physician-Coat changes tack, sympathetic again, "Remember what we discussed yesterday? *Those remains in the morgue, that is not your friend. Your friend's right here with you.*"

Frustration goes maximal. Jech bolts upright. "Listen you quack!" He's getting louder. "You've got someone stuck in one of your death drawers down there who can't get out!"

Coat notices staff and visitors are uneasy due the outburst. He stands, says hushed, "Why don't we go talk somewhere more private..." He points down the hall.

Jech relents, begrudgingly. "We're wasting time..."

Coat nods. He continues gesturing down the hallway as they walk past various concerned hospital visitors.

Jech stares at the floor as they walk, exasperated, saying meekly, "He can't get out of there..."

"And he doesn't need to Mr. Jech." They enter an alcove. "He's dead, and the sooner you accept that the better. They have counselors on staff if you need to talk to someone."

"I'm not crazy."

"Of course not. But in situations like these, it's excusable to be less than rational. Ask yourself, if someone were alive in one of our cold drawers, don't you think the morgue attendant would have heard him?" Exasperation turns a little desperate. Physician-Coat continues. "They're very diligent Mr. Jech. It's not because they're numb to death that they do the job they do. They do the job they do because they value life so much, they believe even those who've lost it deserve respect and dignity. Think about it. There's no one alive in those drawers."

Logic's unassailable but he's not done. Confidence isn't shattered yet. One last thing. One last question. One last hope...

"Who cremated him? Who flipped the switch? I need to make sure he's still alive—"

"Doctor Lytrall is dead."

"No! The person who started the cremation process!"

"Mr. Jech, *I* started the process."

Nothing's left now save a crushing. It slumps him slipping down the wall, unbalanced, like he's tried for a chair pulled out from him though he's tried at nothing. Nothing's left.

Coat catches him under the arms, props him halfway up though no less sunk. Gets him steady at least. Puts a hand on his shoulder as though of accountability. Tries assuring him. "It's protocol. It's old-fashioned," Coat says. "But it's protocol. It dictates that, short of any family or power of attorney present, the person who declared time of death must initiate any interment processes... I'm sorry. He's gone."

JECH'S GOT HIS LEGS BUT the wall's still crutch. He gets himself upright along it as best he can. Physician-Coat's hand squeezes his shoulder now not to assure, to comfort.

Jech's eyes narrow at him. "How is it you're..."

Coat stares quizzically, waits for him to finish.

Doesn't. He turns toward Major Trauma, to where he said goodbye to Dr. Lytrall. Head lowers. It's over. "You're right. If there was somebody alive down there... There can't be."

"That's right," says Coat.

"Right." Jech echoes, not even aware he's doing so.

"Now, about those councilors—"

"No."

"It would only be to your benefit—"

"No. There's still the question of how he knew the gimmick cancelled out."

"Mr. Jech..."

"If he's really dead, he couldn't have known. Yet he wouldn't guess and he wouldn't lie."

"He was in a tremendous amount of distress—"

"Then he would have chose silence. Easiest thing in the world for him: saying no more words than necessary. He was meticulous with language. Exact. *Too* exact."

"Could be I misheard. It was chaos—"

"You misheard something as arcane as *the gimmick cancels out*? Oh, The Professor said it alright. And you heard it."

"I—"

"You said you were the attending *doctor*. Interesting phrasing. Not *physician*? Are you a medical doctor?"

"Now, Mr. Jech—"

"He said it alright. Did you see him say it? His face?"

"I have had just about enough—"

"He wouldn't lie. He said it. You heard it. Were two people involved in this exchange?"

"Listen—"

"He wouldn't lie. You're a doctor. Not a physician?"

"That's right."

"He wouldn't lie. You declared time of death, though not that kind of death. Conceptual death. Toll Lytrall is *gone*?"

"That's right."

"He wouldn't lie. My friend's not in that morgue. Then again, neither are you?"

"*That's right*," says Coat, a little deeper, a little gruffer, a little insistent.

That's what? Jech looks at the doc, curious. Curious resolve?

Coat's got both hands on Jech's shoulders now. A familiar embrace.

Got his legs, gets his balance. Jech moves from the wall, ending the embrace in the process. It was never a curious resolve in him *just* resolve... "I don't think my friend is *down there*. I think that *The Professor* is gone…" He defies any and all grief yet is careful to betray anything more.

"Keep thinking Jech. You're almost there."

Smirks a little. "He's gone. Gone from that morgue… But not far."

"He isn't far is he?"

"Like you said…"

Physician-Coat smirks too, pulls some chunks of something out from his pockets. Looks like rubber.

"*…He's right here with me.*"

Coat slaps the chunks onto his cheeks and forehead. They're prosthetics it turns out. He smooshes them around and into the right places, transforming himself back into a familiar face.

"Jesus Christ! Professor!" Jech embraces his mentor.

The Professor hugs him back, altering his voice, temporarily, to do an impression of Lytrall, "*That's right old friend.*"

"A regular *Rich Lytrall…*"

"Shhh! Toll Lytrall is a quart of cedar ash in the West Brandon Hospital morgue. Couldn't go on living for much longer anyway. People'd start to notice me not dying."

Jech nods in agreement. Hushes, "But you are alive! And you're young!"

"I'm nearly 10,000 years old…"

"And you've got The Gimmick?"

The Professor steps back, looking both ways. He slaps his hands together, hard. He stands there demonstratively, yellow glow beaming from his palms. Prosthetics barely cling to his face. A couple pieces fall off.

18

FIRST INTERVENTION

We interrupt this program to bring you a breaking report. Channel Five has gained access to a live interview, in progress, with the man purported to have carried out the Fort Bartlett siege. We go now live to Federal Security Agency headquarters.

THE INTERVIEWER SITS OPPOSITE CRIMSON. He faces him in that awkward way television interviewers do. Back contorted, twisted, in a chair turned forty-five degrees away from his interlocutor to allow home audiences the sense of being in on the conversation. We catch the interviewer mid-sentence.

"...So you're saying Mr. Dawkitt..."

Interview's impromptu by the way so there's only one camera controlled by the interviewer himself. Interviewer speaks into an older unidirectional microphone but, strange thing, he's also wearing a lapel mic. Other than this oddity, things look like a standard live interview.

"Naw. What I said was—"

"But a person like you... Who's done what you've done, that was clearly your intent."

"You askin' me what my intentions are, or are you simply tellin' me what my intentions—"

"You're getting defensive."

Crimson doesn't look annoyed by the boorishness. He should, but he doesn't. He just leans his cold form closer to the interviewer, says matter-of-factly, "Now, are we gonna, at any point, have a civil conversation? Or ya gonna keep interruptin' me?" He pushes down on the interviewer's microphone, real subtle.

Interviewer swallows hard. Must have let a desire to control public perception get the better of him? One-eighty now though.

"S—Sorry."

Crim stops pushing.

Interviewer wrenches the mic up several more inches, wrapping both hands around it. He collects himself, stifles the obvious nerves and continues. "Why... Why the FSA?"

"The pow'r," Crim says like it's the most obvious answer in the world. *Pow'r* comes out of him like a wild animal roaring it in paradoxical hush.

The interviewer attempts an interpretation. "*Information is power* power? FSA intelligence?"

"Naw. FSA's just the playbill. So I know where to find the mightiest of your country's cast of characters."

"That's... That's just the president... Why not, *um*, go to the White House?"

"Who's sayin' that's not comin' next?" Crimson smiles a wry but calculated smile. No joy in it. His face snaps back to his default. Maybe there's joy in that, who can tell. "I didn't go to your president's house because I'm sure the second I set foot on his front lawn someone'd of whisked him away to a bunker somewhere right out of the movies. Probably already has," He scoffs. Looks at the camera. "'Besides, what do I want with some old man only good for flipping switches? Your elected, they may have control but they certainly ain't got the pow'r. Pow'r rests where it always has…"

He holds up his left hand, index finger to the sky, others folded, then raises his right hand with all fingers splayed. He twinkles each finger on his right, drawing attention to each digit, then folds those fingers into a fist around the lonely index of his left. He cracks the index' knuckle like wringing a neck. *POOF!* He separates his hands and index is gone.

He recommences drawling on again like he's Rod Steiger in *In the Heat of The Night* minus the moral ambiguity, maximus the valium…

"Your leaders…" He looks contemplative a second. "They're like… A child… Child in a rusted-out busted-out ol' wagon. Full of people rollin' on up the road thinkin' they family. Uppity child, temperamental, bossy, who you appease by stakin' a wooden wheel to a pallet t' spin. To steer. Illusion of drivin' keeps him quiet.

"That was the arrangement. Give the power-hungry that illusion. The illusion of importance. Of necessity itself. Keep all brakes on in the world if you know what's good for ya. Keep 'em from making a mess while those who make the world happen do the driving. Good deal. Good deception. Only, somewhere along the way. Along the years. The generations. That uppity little snot toddler got to singin'. Singin' some ungodly lullaby lullin' just enough of you into takin' that carriage in whatever direction l'il leader spins on that dead wheel! While the rest of you all just sat there dumb-founded dumb. Not obliging what should have been the first impulse. Not immediately taking the appeasers of *a mere child* out the driver's seat!"

"Natrally that carriage's just goin' nowhere now. Lucky for you it's not going *nowhere* off a cliff only circles. Dropping you *the people* off where you been picked up and picking you up where you been dropped while *all the while* that child sings you that lullaby about sometime getting to somewhere important... Arriving any minute. Lulling you as you just get on, get off, get on, get off. Like digging a hole to bury your dirt. An' lord help ya if ya don't sing along with the brat!

"Some *a'* your children, your elected, even fool enough to be lulled themselves! Acting like they doing somethin' of a monumental good. Like they taking that carriage to the promised land. Like they saving the world goin' in them circles!

"*Saving the world...* Ought to be a mental illness to believe you can, ought to be a crime to try. No one who's ever saved the world set out to do it and no one who ever set out to do it did anything other than make a mess. *Ought. To. Be. A. Crime!*

"Delusion or no, leaders just children only good for spinning a neutered wheel, flipping dead switches, moving nothin' nobody don't move for 'em. Sure! Baby in control now, but should the people ever wise up *n'* decide to stop appeasing *baby*, that's it. That's all it'll take. That's all it'll be.

"Imagine though. And I mean *imagine*. Paint the picture in y' head. Imagine the people *really* wise up. Wise up and after realizing they never needed baby, they realize they never needed that rotten carriage either! Well hell, they'll squeeze it till the tires pop, burn it to the ground and hail a cab home for all they please. No stopping 'em. Tiny body of tiny-bodied bureaucrats can't stop the masses. Not the bureaucrats not even their police. Whatcha think copper gonna do when the neighbor he cracking the skull of says, *kill me and there's no food on your family's table... You think the Prime Minister can farm?* That's it. That's all it'll ever be.

"That's what pow'r really is. *Disposition to control.* To have as much control as you want, for as long as you want, over as many objects, earthly or other, as you can dream.

"Damned-foolest thing of all of this disposition is, for whatever reason... And there's got to be a reason... Those of the only real pow'r stifle themselves of it. Cede it. Give it to the babies. Delude themselves that even if they don't need the driver they need the carriage and the carriage needs the driver. It's just another wheel for 'em. Many wheels in the people's lives they completely unaware's taking them nowhere but to one... Damned-foolest of things.

"Flat tire, dead battery, seized engine grinding away on fumes, rust rust rust, and what do they do? Get out and walk? Naw! They tell themselves the solution to all their problems is: Find a better *baby* to spin that wheel! For whatever why, the people neuter themselves... All of 'em. Cedin'... Sittin'.

He looks back to the interviewer for his recapitulation. "Your leader's just an appeased little child of the benighted. Your leader's all leaders. Legion. Flippers of dead switches if they good for anything at all and I got no use for that."

"S—So, what you're saying is—"

"It's the people I intend to wrest pow'r from cuz that's where the pow'r's always been. And, unlike the armies pow'r-less to stop even a fifth of your people should they revolt, all five hundred million of your citizens, riding in on the backs of those armies for all I care, could come at me guns a blazin' and I could kill every single one of them just by sittin' in my rocking chair. Easy pickins.

"All I want to know is, where y'all are, what ya capable of, and how that suits me." He holds up a tablet with the FSA logo on it and information flashing by on the screen. He looks back to the interviewer. "Now, why don't we start with you? What *use* are you to someone like me?"

He's caught the interviewer off guard.

"Um... I... I."

"*Um, um, um. I, I, I.* You think your *use* to me comes in the form of you borin' me boy? It sure don't come in the form of you putting words in my mouth, thoughts in my head, and values in my character like ya been all night." He leans back in his chair. "Naw, you had your chance. *You. Are. Useless. To. Me.*"

He pulls out that pistol of his. He points it at the interviewer. The interviewer's eyes widen. He fires.

SPLOOSH.

A spritz of water hits the interviewer in the face causing the microphone to drop. Interviewer bolts for the door. It won't open. A slight whirring sound is evident.

Crimson faces the camera again, "Ha! Ain't that crackin'? Ain't. That. A. Scream?" Wavers the water pistol a little. "All those dead men out there, killed themselves for fear of a bath."

FROM THE TV SCREEN WE see Crimson. He gets up out of his interview chair, taking off his coat as he rises. Turns out he's been wearing a noose under there. He looks to his audience.

"Better get to provin' yo'selves Amerika."

Under the interviewer's chair we see a winch has been set in gear by the releasing of that microphone. Winch is whirring away pulling a rope attached to Crim's noose. Rope rises behind him as the noose constricts around his neck. It loses all slack and, just as he's lifted off the ground, he throws his coat over the camera.

Through the blank screen we hear the sound of the interviewer choking and struggling for air, then... Test pattern.

JECH, THE PROFESSOR, NAND, AND Etty stand around the proscenium, test pattern behind them sounding like tinnitus.

"We know his *ends*..." The Professor says. "...As if we needed to ask. Now, what are the *means*?"

"Set your watch he'll have Jane there to dig him out of any fuck-ups," Nand volunteers.

"Yes... Jane..." The Professor's pacing, like he's in front of his class again. "But Crimson is too meticulous to allow for any 'fuck-ups'."

"Jane's a living breathing *fuck-up*."

"I stand corrected then." He stops, eyes look up and to the left. Eyes narrow. "Jane's involvement also means Crimson knows about you Jech."

Jech nods.

Nand's resolved to something, "We should do some reconnoitering. Get a peek at the Risk board. I wanna know how many of Jane's men are in that place and where."

THE INTERVENTIONISTS CAMP OUT ON the helicopter pad of a high-rise northwest of FSA headquarters. They're using various spotting scopes, binoculars, and the like. Nand's the only one tending to his scope at this point. Everyone else seems to have grown bored. Nand's also enamored with a little scratch pad. There're stick figures and strange coding drawn all over it. He scribbles vigorously between peeks through the scope.

The Professor glances at the scratchpad. "Your eyes full Mr. Nand?"

"Just about."

"What can you tell us?"

"Just what I thought. Jane's copied a page right out of my playbook... Literally." He rolls over and pulls another notepad out of his waistband. "Here's my playbook." He holds a page of it up. "And here's the positions, movement, and assignments of Jane's men." He points to the scratchpad he's been scribbling on. Pages are identical. "Only thing I don't know is Crimson's location."

"He's not going to follow any patterns," The Professor warns.

Jech sits himself up to get comfortable. He's sitting criss-cross applesauce now. "Too bad we couldn't just bring the whole building down on top of—"

"Get flat boy!" Nand pulls our hero back supine. "Got an anomaly here." He's barking as he peers through his scope. "Looks like Jane's gone off book. Sniper, hotel roof, *tally check right 45 lazy 30.*"

"What?" Everyone else on their scopes now.

Nand, aggravated, "Down and to the right."

From the point of view of a scope, we see a sniper and scout prone on a hotel roof west of Fort Bartlett. They're facing the FSA building.

"No joy," Nand relents. "These guys are government boys." He moves his scope. "Oh, look at this..." A group of armed men moves in formation toward the rear gate. Using the trees for cover, they wait. "SEALs. They're going for it."

"That's a bad idea…" says The Professor as…

PSG1 drops to Nand's side.

Jech bursts into a sprint from out the group and leaps off the helipad so high and far he leaves the roof completely. He drops below its edge and disappears.

Nand gets into position with the PSG1. Butt to shoulder, finger on grip. Rifle's bipod pops down. Rubber feet root in the asphalt. Don't know why but he has some sort of affinity *better* an inkling. He lifts the weapon up ever so slightly in his firing hand—impressed. "Light… What's the range on this thing?"

Prof looks away from his binoculars a second. "Baltimore."

THE SEAL SNIPER AND HIS scout lay on the hotel roof doing as trained. Sniper's aim is on a balaclava'd guard manning a mini-gun turret at the fort gate.

Radio Chatter squawks back and forth.

We breach on your go Echo 5.

Sniper moves his right index finger from grip to trigger. Aims. Crosshairs stop solid on mini-gun guard.

Sniper fires.

Balaclava fuzz puffs as guard collapses, falling out of sight.

"Nice shot," offers scout, eyes still on his scope.

Echo 4, Echo 5 maintain overwatch.

From the scout's scope we see the SEAL team creeping closer to the gate.

Overwatch, can I get a SitRep?

Nothing.

What's the status on that SitRep overwatch?

Scout's eyes remain on scope. "Gonna answer 'em man?"
Still nothing.
Scout checks to see what's up, looks over to his partner.
Sniper's head is sunken and there are spots of blood under his trigger. Scout shakes him. Gunman rolls over dead. Scout removes his helmet to reveal a head blown open. Angle of entry/exit suggests another sniper above at two O'clock.

Shock on the face of scout for a second. *Shock* comes from the hardwiring, can't help it. His *sense of duty* comes from the training. Duty's slower, can't help that either. He gets there though, fast as he can. He doesn't need to look up, it's all blue sky. Angle's impossible and he knows it. Angle's impossible from behind too and there're no angles left. Nevertheless, he grabs his partner's rifle and slinks to the roof exit.

THE SEAL TEAM IS JUST creeping up to the rear gate as the scout bursts out on comms,

Echo 5 is down! Repeat, Echo 5 is down! Shooter in area, location unknown.

Team can barely react, when...
The guard that Echo 5 took out pops up alive as ever because he's Crimson. Somehow he's pure apathy and

beaming at the same time, hands latched onto his mini-gun joysticks. SEALs scramble for a cover that isn't there. Crim's about to fire when... Jech pops up alive as ever too but we've got no reason to doubt *his* vitality. He's not emotionless just beaming. He's standing just inches from the mini-gun muzzle maintaining a *don't you do it* posture as the SEALs continue running for cover. His beam diminishes slightly as he ponders Crim. Ponders over this first face-to-face out-the-bottle.

"You were more alive behind that glass," he says in curiosity.

Here's how much Crim's interested in chitchat: *BRAAAAAP!*

He opens the gun up wide. Column of muzzle flair erupts. Casings fly everywhere. The shootin' barrel sashays left, right, up, down, all around and back again. He fires like there's music in it as Jech keeps up with the flair, staying between the blast and the SEALs allowing them to get to that cover. Crim can't shake him.

SQUAWK! Midas is in threat circle. Midas is shooter. Fall back. Do not engage. Repeat, fall back. Do not engage.

Final movement comes to a crescendo. Crim's fingers ease off the triggers as the glare of the muzzle becomes the ripple of The Gimmick. Naturally Jech's chest bursts glow after absorbing those rounds but so does Crim's. *The Gimmick cancels out.*

What's Crim thinking about the man who foiled his attack? Who's surely the guy Lytrall warned would *stop him*? Heavy stuff though Crim looks back in the bottle. Like he never left. Demeanor hasn't changed a wink. Not at all save for, maybe, the slightest of clenching of teeth.

It's his trigger finger that betrays his true feelings:

BRAAAAAP!

He opens the gun up a second time only with muzzle fixed.

The bullets rip a yellow glow out of Jech's chest. Crim's too. Bullets bore right through that glow and hit what's behind. Not the SEALs though. Jech's intervention allowed a sufficient window for EVAC.

Crimson spends all remaining rounds with this second burst and before the barrels can even stop spinning he launches himself onto his counterpart. He's on Jech's hips, tearing into him and gouging with a speed and unpre-dictability that leaves his opponent defenseless. Jech tries his best to get any kind of upper-hand but the villain's too wily.

The beating goes on as Jane and nine of his henchmen move toward the gate. Some of his men hold M4s, some hold Codas. Jane holds a Marlboro between his teeth.

"Nets on hostile. Fire on my go," he shouts.

Coda mercs ready their weapons on Jech, awaiting the order. Then...

BIM!

A gob of plasma is already drying on Jane's forehead as he goes down convulsing, lightning flashing all about him.

Nand smirks, puts finger on trigger once more for good measure.

A now supine Jane struggles to lift himself, cigarette smoldering on the ground beside. Just as his wobbly head with its slack jaw gets perpendicular to torso... *BIM!* Another gob of plasma bursts through that slack jaw running right down his throat. He hiccups then convulses some more.

BIM! BIM! BIM! Nand lets loose on the CODA mercs

now. One shot one spill. They topple like Jane *sans* lozenge. A couple of the still-standing mercs reach for the dropped net guns. *BANG! BANG! BANG!* Sniper Scout took those shots, hitting all three of the turfed CODAs. A couple of them fire off their mesh spinning themselves on the ground like tops. The other's split in two. All are out of commission.

Back to the fracas...

Crim's still on top gouging away but Jech's got the timing. It's a stochastic rhythm so any prediction of any move's going to be probabilistic, a roll of a die. If he can just... *SNATCH!* Got it! He's caught Crim's right wrist in his left hand. Holds onto it with Beowulf's grip. He pops off a couple rights and Crim's hold loosens on hips. Knees come through the gap and Jech wraps his legs around villain's trunk. Grabs back onto that wrist putting Crim in a triangle choke.

More Glow.

Mercs squint through the amber, see that Jech has the upper-hand. Their leader's out cold too. They have no choice.

"Fall back! Fall the fuck back! Somebody grab Jane!"

These orders appear to activate Crimson. Glow intensifies even more. He plants his left hand in the dirt and pushes himself up. He can't break free of Jech's grip on his right arm but he can move against the force of that grip. *This ain't no Rio Bravo arm wrastlin' tourney...* He drives his right hand toward his opponent's neck with a power unimaginable, unstoppable. He claws his fingers into Jech's throat, behind his windpipe, tickling the carotid and jugular. Literally tickling them. Crim's a freak. Then... He closes his grip with a clenching *CRUNCH!* Gimmick pours out of both of those tickled arteries. Jech's got next to nothing left. He's choking on his own glow and impossibly overpowered. He just lets his head flop back and tries tightening that triangle hold. Buys himself back the slightest of leverage but now he's really got nothing left.

Crim smiles that plastic smile. "Thanks brotha. Was countin' on your caress." He pulls Jech up using the man's windpipe as handle. He stands now, his opponent hanging off his torso a second, then... He spins. The centripetal force causes the already spent Jech just enough queasiness to loosen all remaining holds. Two more slingshot spins for momentum and Crim lets fly slamming Jech to the ground with a *SMASH!*

What to do now but walk away? Crim's goin' home, his back to a billowing mushrooming glow. Glow unfolds outward, wrapping inward at the same time, spending itself. *He really hurt ya Jech.* Glow cashes out completely as Crim moves through the gate. Then... He stops, his face still tollbooth operator indifferent. His arms are expressive enough. Elbows on hips, forearms extended, palms up. Fingers flutter on each hand. He's welcoming something when...

SWOOSH!

Jech pops up behind wrapping his arms around Crim's torso at forty-five-degree angles this time. Crimson immediately begins finagling and twisting. Jech holds tighter but his opponent's strength reserves are no match for him in any state letalone this one. Crim easily manages to turn himself one-eighty. He faces Jech in his arms. Strangest hug you've ever seen. He unleashes a smile that's no smile at all. He gnashes teeth.

CHOMP! CHOMP!

One of those gnashing teeth lights up like an LED.

FLASH! FLASH! FLASH!

Confused by this, Jech gives Crim an accidental inch. Crim leans back and opens his coat like he's been waiting his whole life to do it. It's a bomb vest on our now gloating villain.

FLASH! FLASH! KABOOM!

Explosion sends Jech flying out into the street and Crimson everywhere else. The entrance to the fort is rubble.

19

THE PUBLIC SECTOR

Crack of light emerges from what was pure dark moments ago.

"There he is," we hear from some voice out the black.

More cracks of light punch through. What turns out to be a large chunk of debris is lifted off of Jech as EMS workers dig him out from twisted metal, splintered wood, and pulverized cinder block. They drag him out of a sufficiently enlarged opening in the rubble and up onto his feet. Slight glow subsides from his dusty bod.

As quick as he's upright...

POOSH!

He's netted. He struggles. *POOSH!* He's netted again. He topples to the ground.

"Keep Greatest American Hero here standing."

Feds swarm in to follow the orders of the man with the suit and dark glasses. They inch Jech up by the nets and move him to his partners in crime. Nand, Etty, and The Professor have been detained too it turns out. Suit-Man surveys the Interventionists. He points a finger at The Professor.

"This one too. He's one of 'em."

POOSH!

TEAM INTERVENTIONIST MEMBERS SIT CUFFED to an interview table in an 'undisclosed location'. Undisclosed but inferable. They were bussed there in a minivan with no blindfolds and the sunroof open for christ's sake! It's down the road from a Staples. Anyway...

Suit-Man enters the interview room.

He moves behind Jech, grabbing onto the back of his chair. "Up."

"What?"

Suit-Man rips the chair out from under him sending his ass to the floor. No gimmick as Suit-Man's broken any fall with his foot.

He says again, "Up."

Jech gets up.

Suit-Man takes the chair to the opposite side of the table and plops down on it. Guess Jech's standing for the proceedings?

Suit looks these vigilantes over a second, then...

"Fuckin' Crimson Dawkitt's a real trip ain't he?" Real turn to jovial. Standard MO. "Trickster and a half! London police boys swear they've seen him eat styrofoam and gasoline just so he can piss napalm!" Suit focuses on Jech again. "What would you say if I told ya last week I thought you were good for the London Culling?"

"I'd say you're a dummy if you do yet."

Suit-Man erupts with laughter.

Jech isn't amused. "Who are you?"

"He's a fed," Nand says.

"You know him?"

"Something oozes out the dirt in the rain I gotta know him to know he's a worm?"

Suit-Man seems to be enjoying this. "Boys ya flatter me. But let's talk turkey bones. Your escapades have caught the attention of the United States Government."

Etty makes an *oh no* face.

"Our saving lives you mean?" The Professor suggests. "Just tell us what punitive measures you have in store."

"*Punitive measures*? Why not just say 'punishment'. Are all your kind so pretentious?"

"Academics?"

Suit laughs. "Oh, touch! Love this guy!"

"*Touch*?"

"Coulda said *touché* but I'm not pretentious that way." Suit's conciliatory suddenly, "You think I'm here to bust ya? Naw, you're not in any trouble."

Etty looks relieved. He tries to wipe his brow. His restraints stop him... *HEY!*

Suit-Man continues, "On the contrary. Why do you think I'm so pissy right now? Much as it pains me to do it, I'm here to inform you guys that, *AHEM*... The United States Government is fully prepared to provide you with whatever resources you need should you agree to help apprehend Crimson Dawkitt."

"We'll take it," The Professor accepts with zero hesitation.

"What?" Jech protests.

"We'll take it," The Professor reiterates. He hunkers down and pulls the team close to him though he speaks directly to Jech. "We don't have a choice. Crimson is full of endless sleazy tricks and we gotta beat him at his own game.

We need a few sleazy tricks of our own and there's no better place to find them than Government."

All but Jech sit in agreement. Jech *is* in agreement though—just can't sit...

"We'll take it."

ALL STAND IN A GOVERNMENT issued lab facility of that same undisclosed location that must be next to a Subway franchise or something because everything smells like stale bread and bioluminescent roast beef... Lab's completely bare save for silver surfaces, some chairs, bit of stationary, and a desk or two. It's a little less confining than the interrogation room... There's a knock at the door.

Jech opens it to reveal Simmons on the other side. "Simone..." he says warmly.

"Hiya Rogee," She says in playfulness and equal warmth. "Doc said I should come by..." She flips up a laminate clinging to her left breast pocket. *Level 5* security clearance is indicated on it. "...To chronicle what you guys are up to."

Jech looks to The Professor. Professor looks back with a *so you don't lose touch of the 'why's'* look. Jech puts an arm around Simmons' shoulder and she wraps her arms around his midsection. They walk into the lab acting like their lovey-dovey bullshit is as professional as can be."

"Hello! Hello!" Suit-Man barges in past Simmons and Jech, blowing through the place, struttin' smugly. "And what do we all think of the new lab?"

"I think it's empty," says The Professor.

"Yeah, we're working on that list a' yours..."

Nand stands next to a whiteboard and some markers, like he couldn't be happier in his own stone-faced way. Like the whiteboard and markers are all he needs.

"We got a whiteboard and markers. I couldn't be happier. Got all I need." He draws out little stickmen like he's a football coach at half-time.

Suit-Man focuses on The Professor. "About that list. One item just says *voyager*. What's that?"

"Voyager," is the answer. "I want a spacecraft capable of leaving our solar system entirely. The faster the better."

"Why?"

"Gonna put Crimson in it."

Suit-Man reacts in plastic glee, "Ha! Shoot 'em into outta space! Love it! You gimmick freaks certainly got a sense a' fuckin' humor!"

Professor smiles one of those slightly crooked smiles that suggests he doesn't appreciate being patronized. Hint of concession in it though. It might just fool a government boy, say, into thinking he's won some sort of battle now, realize the rebuke later.

Suit fails to catch anything anyway, barrels on. "We got some experimental tech just waiting for a couple a' stupid guinea pigs to test it! Super-fast stuff. Shouldn't be a problem." Suit-Man says this as he glances over to Simmons. Another shift, "What's *Film at Eleven* doing here? I didn't approve of that!"

Simmons frowns at Suit-Man.

Professor intervenes. "Oh but you did. *Any resource we need*, remember..."

Simmons shrugs a *wha-ya gonna do now fed* shrug.

Suit softens again like he could give a shit, "Ha, *touch!*" He's inching for the facility door. "Look, I gotta shoot your list up the chain of command. Get approval. Fill out some forms. Ya know... You'll have your stuff lickety-split." He's half out that door as he says those last few words, like he doesn't want anyone else to get a word in. He stops himself leaving however, as though remiss, gets somber. "Bless you weirdos for your service to the great people of these United States of Amerika's Government."

Now Suit-Man's gone. No one's sad to see him go.

Jech shakes his head. "Leave it to the Government to turn stopping a supervillain into a trip to the DMV."

Prof concurs. "No point denying it. We work in the public sector now."

Jech adds, "Where the bureaucracy is free and the checks keep coming no matter how much we fuck up."

"We should get some work done."

"Yep. Time to get to work."

...

...

"Wanna get a sandwich?"

"Sure."

WE'RE WIDE ON THE FOUR of the five interventionists sitting around a seminar table—table covered in sandwich wrappers—as the fifth continues adding little stick men to his whiteboard.

Time passes.

SAME WIDE SHOT AS LAST but the sandwich wrappers are gone and there are more stickmen on Nand's board.

Time passes.

SAME WIDE SHOT AS LAST but even more stickmen on Nand's board.

Time passes.

· · ·

SAME WIDE SHOT AS LAST but **Simmons** is working on her laptop and **Nand** is erasing some stickmen so he can replace them with different stickmen.

Time passes.

IN AN ATTEMPT TO END the boredom, everyone but Nand— still at the board—has entered into casual conversation. The Professor speaks insistently.

"I'm telling you, it's true. *Men who live on the sun are cold as ice.*"

Etty nods in agreement. Jech scoffs. Simmons types.

"That's ridiculous!" Jech laughs.

"Why's it ridiculous?" Professor feigns indignation.

"Well for one, it came out of the mouth of a philosopher. For two, and brace yourself for this: Nobody. Lives. On. The. Sun."

Prof rebuts, "What if I said, *men who live on the sun burn to a crisp*? Is that true?"

"Of course."

"I thought *nobody lives on the sun...*"

"But, if you *did* live on the sun you'd be burnt to a crisp, not cold."

"How do you know? You check everybody who's ever lived on the sun?"

"There's nobody to check!"

"So, how do you know?"

He relents ever so slightly, "I guess I don't for sure. Though I'd *sure* bet on it."

"But, with the statement *men who live on the sun burn to a crisp*, I'm saying something like, *no man has met the first condi-*

tion: ie living on the sun, and failed to meet the second: ie burning to a crisp. Right?"

Jech's a little suspicious now, "I guess..."

"And also, when it comes to *men who live on the sun being cold as ice*, no man has met the first condition: living on the sun, and failed to meet the second: being cold as ice. Right?"

"Right, because no man has met the first condition..."

"So how would you prove me wrong?"

"Huh?"

"Let's use a simplified example. How would you prove me wrong if I said *all men who live in West Brandon are right-handed*?

"No tricks?"

"No tricks."

"I'd find a person living in West Brandon who's left-handed."

"Because to be left-handed is to *not* be right-handed?"

"Right."

"Exactly! To falsify any 'all men...' claim, you only need provide a single example of a man meeting the first condition but failing to meet the second. Like living in West Brandon and not being right-handed. Right?"

"Right."

"Conversely, if you ran through a list of all men who've ever lived and *didn't* find a single one *both* living in West Brandon and not being right-handed, you'd have to conclude the claim true. Right?"

"Right."

"But you could run through a list of all people who've ever lived and you wouldn't find a single one *both* living on the sun and who's *not* cold as ice. Right?"

"Right."

"Where you'd have to find at least one sun-dweller who's not cold for my claim to be false?"

"*Right...*"

"And you wouldn't find even a single one?"

"*Riiiight...*"

"So by your own standard my statement's not false and, if it's not false, it's true! My statement's true. I'm right."

Etty nods. Simmons types. Nand sketches. Jech sits looking like a man bracing for the smell that follows a gurgling sink to tell the nature of the problem only the smell don't come. Then...

"Hey!" He shouts.

"Ha!"

Hero shakes his head. He's been had. Talk of what is or isn't true reminds him of something else to be settled. "Alright, wanna talk *truth* Socrates? Is anything you told me about my past true?"

Etty remains transfixed. Nand continues to strategize. Simmons glances up from her laptop though continues typing. A little faster evidently.

Professor doesn't hesitate. "Everything except that nonsense about *induced quantum entanglement*."

"You didn't make yourself in a lab?"

"Didn't make you in a lab either. Though you *were* made." He gets matter of fact. "This is what I know: we've got The Gimmick, we don't die, microwaves knock us out, and on certain conditions we can replicate."

"And what conditions are those?"

"I'll tell you on my deathbed."

He smiles. "No more secrets after that?"

Professor smiles back. "Jech, that's the last secret I'll ever have to tell you."

Everyone's enjoying this little moment when...

"Alright!" Suit-Man's arrived and is announcing it to the world. "Got you guys everything ya asked for. In the trucks. Even the goddamn spaceship."

Everyone looks surprised that any of this even happened at all. Then...

"Ya gonna help unload it?"

20

COMMUNICATION BREAKDOWN

overnment Laboratory – Ballistics: Undisclosed Location.

An M2 Browning machine gun sits pointed at the head of a man made entirely of ballistics gel. The Professor stands next to *Gel-Man* playing with a small green panel of something, flexing it in his hands. It looks like a piece of teflon for a barbecue grill, only green.

Nand and Jech stand on the opposite side of some plexiglass meant to protect them from the heavy artillery.

"Got something that might come in handy." Nand reaches into his equipment bag. "It's not exactly Professor Brand technology, but it's helped me out of a few jams." He finds what he's been searching for. Reveals it.

"Air duster?"

"For when you need a clean conscience." He winks. He *is* holding a tiny can of compressed air. The kind for cleaning components. Jech's skeptical. Nand notices. "For breaking out of restraints." He slips the canister up his sleeve and puts himself in a pair of handcuffs. He then demonstrates the process. Canister slips out via gravity and he finagles it in his hands. He turns the canister upside down and blanches a link in the chain of the cuffs with liquid CO_2. It's frosty. He yanks on the chains in both directions and Mr. Frosty shatters. "Learn to do this behind your back. No trick too many when it comes to Dawkitt."

Jech nods, takes the spray.

"Ready fellas?"

PROFESSOR STANDS AT THE head of Gel-Man positioning the green panel around the face of it. Jech and Nand observe under glass. Prof finishes his task and doubles back to the machine gun.

He wastes no time. He chunks the slide, takes the trigger bars in hands, and *BANG! BANG! BANG!*... Slams multiple .50 cal rounds into the face of Gel-Man. He disables the M2 and waves Nand and Jech over to the experiment.

HE'S WHIPPING THE PANEL OFF Gelly as the pair gets to him. No damage to dummy's face whatsoever. Professor tosses the panel to Nand, revealing that it too is none-the-worse-for-wear.

"Strong enough a man can walk away from an antipersonnel round, thin enough he'd detect a shot from a daisy rifle."

Nand would be impressed if there wasn't a more pressing concern. "Doc..."

"Yes?"

He points at The Professor's abdomen. Three large glowing holes slowly fade on his midsection.

Professor looks down, looks up. "Oh yes! The material is highly elastic. I recommend not getting within ten yards of anyone wearing this iteration. Should have the kinks worked out in short order."

JECH'S WATCHING SIMMONS ON THE proscenium television. She's finishing a report. He's not staring at her like a complete dope, but he's certainly staring at her with all he's got. Rank sentimentalist.

Despite our armed forces' recent failed attempts at recapturing FSA headquarters, true to form, Brandon East's local hero's timely interventions have saved dozens of lives in those attempts.

"Quite the girl," says The Professor approaching the stage. "Rosalind Russell will have to play her in the movie."

Jech's nodding in agreement but realizes something. "What year do you think this is ya big fat lummox?"

"News report on worth watching? The distant past..."

But Jech's no longer listening. He's back to fixating on his girl Friday. Happiness fades a little though. As often happens, warm thoughts of a loved one turn to concern for well-being, then to fear of diminishment of that well-being, then thoughts of how to prevent that diminishment. There's a war on doncha know? Of sorts... But no solace. No solutions currently.

"What is it?" The Professor asks.

"He's stronger than I thought. Smarter too."

Professor thinks a second. Resolve. "All I can tell you is, when things are at their bleakest, don't let him see your pain. This, I assure you Roger, is no platitude."

"Just suck it up and move forward?"

"There'll be a direction, not sure which. No platitude."

He puzzles over the arcane advice. Comprehension rears as...

FLILIILILILIILILIL... The projector's fired up. Sound's blaring and images flicker and flash on the screen. It's Charles Bronson.

You make sounds like you're a mean little ass kicker...

"Who the hell's up there?" Jech shouts.

...You keep talking, I'm going to take your head off.

He and The Professor start up the center aisle. Jech glances to his right as he goes. It's Crimson. He focuses his attention back to the screening room exit and... *Crimson!* He double-takes. It *is* Crimson, big as life, lounging in a theater seat, enjoying the show as much as he can enjoy anything. Killer cocks his head at the pair. There's acknowledgment in his eyes, intention too, little else.

FLILIILILILIILILILIP! and the projector cuts out...

"Lock the doors!" Jech shouts as he moves to his counterpart.

Crim rises as though good manners dictate he do so. Jech gets just close enough and Mr. Decorum opens his coat. Another bomb vest. Jech stops. Eyes narrow. He's running some kind of calculus. No output. What's this guy up to?

"Running out of ideas Crimson or just wardrobe?"

"I don't have to detonate this you know..." Says this suggestive, real thick. He waves a smartphone.

"You giving me an ultimatum?"

"Jech." The Professor tries.

But Jech barrels on, "Newsflash asshole, you could go supernova and we're all walking outta here just fine!"

"Jech!" Prof grips him by the shoulder. Jech turns.

"What?"

"That's *not* what he means."

Crim's head tilts. He gets a look of recognition. Like bumping into a coworker on vacation but it's recognition all the same. "Is that... Is that you pappy? Pappy still alive? Well don't that take the bear shit out the buckwheat!" He smiles plastic.

The Professor ignores him, keeps his focus on Jech. "If someone else sets off that ve—"

"He's right Jech. Pappy's always been 'head the curve." Crim pulls the vest outward a couple tugs. "See, maybe I detonate this thing or maybe the person on the other end of this phone does." He's wiggling the device. "I coulda' rigged it so they set me to blazes with a *hello*. Maybe I'm waitin' for someone to text me back, answer an email, Google their own name, ego-check, retweet, repost, swipe right, block, mute, quote, DM, stank spank, buy with one click, dislike a clip of some asshole reactin' to his first viewing of *Encino Man* even though ya can't see the dislikes anymore... Whateva' input I please... Then boom!"

Jech gets it. Crim's is a story he understands. It's a dire one, sure, but the implications? Does the gimmick really work that way—

"Don't think I got it in me?" Crim says. He takes out a Glock. Just a Glock. Nothing to these three. None flinch. Glock's got something on its trigger. Looks like a trigger-guard but there's a blinking LED. Gotta be mechanical. Crim tucks it in at the top of his vest. Gun rests with barrel pointed up at his chin. He works at his phone a moment. Holds it out. "Say my name boy."

Jech don't move.

"Say my name."

Then...

"Do it Jech." Professor implores over shoulder. "We need to know."

A beat.

"Fine." He says this craning at Prof. Turns back to pure capitulation... "Crimson Dawkitt."

"LOUDER!" Crim issues the phone nearer.

"CRIMSON DAWKITT!"

Mechanics at the Glock's trigger whirr for a half-second...

BANG!

Hero and villain's heads lurch back simultaneous at mirrored angles. Glow erupts. We've seen it before but never with such meaning. It drips off their chins. Sprays out their crowns. Dissipates.

Experiment's a success.

Crim's back to walking.

A few steps closer and he recommences. Speaks as though in a sidebar. "Any input I please." Any implication he pleases. As... He walks his fingers across the screen of the phone. Then... "Hell, maybe I'm just waitin' on that auda-cious little reporter friend of yours to *reach out and touch me...*"

Crim's is a story he understands.

It's a pressure.

In his chest.

There's tremor too.

The Professor reaches out though stops short of touch.

He gonna help ya or halt ya Jech?

Hero vibrates like quartz. He wants to lunge but knows better but forward back forward back he goes... Red face. Red eyes. Red hot. Rage. Fear. Can he get to Crimson in time to flip that kill switch? Is there a kill switch? Can he get to

Simmons? His face and chest are the kind of hot you know's turning the skin to sunset, a red-bordering-on-purple of twilight until, because he's so damned feverish, the heat brings out the glow.

Can he get to her?

Crim's loving all this. "You look like you wish you could break inna two. A Jech to save the girl. A Jech to tear me to pieces. Pullin' in both directions at once. No different than standin' still..." He recommences walking toward our hero as...

Nand and Etty burst through the screening room doors.

Professor's hand goes up at the two. "No!" He waves them away. *BACK! BACK!* The pair oblige.

Crim keeps walking. He has his phone in clear view as he goes. He stops toe-to-toe with Jech.

"How ya gonna get between me and my quarry now hero?"

Mentor and protege are stone statues at this. Both thinking but again there's no output.

"I'm gonna walk right out that door..." Crim gloats more, "...And the 10,000-year-old philosopher and his apprentice are just gonna let me do it. Not 'head any curve this time old man." He gets extra casual. He strolls past everyone, leaving the screening room and entering the lobby.

All remain still except Jech. He bolts for the side exit leading to the back alley.

"Roger!"

Looks back, shakes his head like he knows he isn't in his right mind but all he has at this point is his path of least resistance and that path doesn't involve standing still.

SIMMONS BARGES INTO HER MANAGING editor's office.

"Take any good shits lately Burgess?"

"What are you on about Simmons?"

"Now that we've passed the Bechdel test, what the fuck is this?" She tosses some pages onto her boss' desk.

Burgess knocks them aside, acts nonchalant. "You one of our interns all of a sudden? You not know copy when you see it?"

"*Vigilante Turned Domestic Terrorist: Masked Flash Storms Fort Bartlett*? You're recontextualizing this? This is my story."

"Your story's tabled Simmons. You should have seen this coming. Vigilante glows, Dawkitt glows. How'd you miss that?"

"Didn't."

"Well how many assholes in this town can I smack around a little then bend over and take to Emerald City?"

RING!

Simmons reaches for her phone...

Any input he pleases...

She turns it to silent mode. She looks a shrewd look of distrust at Burgess. "This your decision?"

"Upstairs. But I didn't fight it."

Phone rumbles in her pocket. Whoever called must be texting or something. She takes it out and... *Any input...* Like an Olympic curler, slides it out the office door. "Fuck it. And fuck you too. I'll go freelance. Shit, I'll start my own outlet. People only watch us for the hero stuff now anyways. You can tell upstairs I quit. Tell 'em too, when they chose me for obedience, they chose wrong."

Burgess chuckles. "You'll calm down. This'll all be okay."

"I mean it Sylvia."

"Then I wish you all the best," Burgess condescends. "Our *desired* audience has never been the type to take to conspiracy theories anyway. Go appease the whackos wanting to hear your tales of secret leagues of heroes and villains."

Simmons can smell the groundwork for character assassination when she sees it. "Where's conspiracy?"

"Huh?"

"Conspiracy... In my stories. Necessary conditions Sylvia. *Two or more parties colluding to achieve some end...* I talk about a *lone* vigilante turned *lone* hero. Hell, where's there any *theory*?"

"Th—Theory... I'm sure I..." Burgess fumfers like she knows she's been caught employing a fallacy she coached Simmons to use herself. Simmons pounces.

"They're called *hypotheses* Sylvia. When are you establishment empty-heads gonna learn nobody buys your screaming 'conspiracy' every time you hear an explanation you don't like? This. Is. Just. So—" The reporter cuts herself off, shakes her head. She's done. "You know what, I'm done. Call me if you ever get into journalism asshole!"

Almost done...

She's already half out the office door when she stops and looks back to Burgess. "For the record, the hero's name is *The Interventionist* not The Masked Flash."

ANY...

SHE BLOWS ACROSS THE office floor. She crashes into her desk waking up the computer on it.

"Fuckin' blue dots." She's opening up each of a list of unopened emails seemingly just to get rid of the 'Unread' notifications.

CLICK... CLICK... CLICK... CLICK...

Her finger hovers over the mouse button, cursor on an

email with the words 'Don't Miss!' in the subject line when...

"You know you can just click the *mark all* button," says Jerry Garber, weatherman at-large, looking over his shoulder. He turns away again, adding in hushed rebuke, "Or, you can actually read your emails..."

She pauses. She smirks a *thanks but no thanks* smirk at the back of his head and...

Clicks on the *Don't Miss* email, when...

A message pops up. It's spam, something about a *24-Hour Flash Sale—huge new deals*....

"Hey Jerry, how do you start a YouTube account?"

"You're an investigative reporter and you don't have a YouTube account? How do you do your research?"

"Shoe leather Jerry. You know or not?"

"I'm busy Simmons."

"Lot of meteorological data on that fantasy football site? Siri, start me a YouTube account!"

Nothing.

"Siri!" She reaches to her empty pocket, realizing what she did with her phone. "Fuckin' phone."

RING!

Is that her landline? They don't ring as much as they used too but in the open concept of her office a collective of ringtones comes often enough, hence a certain ancient cacophony comes often enough. The ringing all runs together when it does. *RING!*

She stops typing, looks around. "Is that me? Thought I logged off the system..."

"Burgess logs you back in every morning," says Jerry. "Something about you shuffle-boarding your phone down the hall one too many times."

"*Nerve,*" Simmons says. "I don't recognize this number. Do you recognize this number? I'm not answering."

"Maybe it's your *boyfriend* the Masked Flash..." Jerry says this like it's the fifth grade.

"Gossiping about a coworker's relationship is sexual harassment Jerry. Read the poster in the break room."

RING!

"Maybe he's asexual?" Jerry says like he's the king of loopholes. "Can't be sexual harassment if there's no *sexual.*"

RING!

"Trust me, he's *not* asexual."

"What's that supposed to... Hey! Innuendo's sexual harassment. Read the poster in the break room."

RING!

"Oh everything's sexual harassment according to that stupid poster!"

But Jerry's not listening. He's put his headphones on to drown out the ring-a-ding-din.

She gives the telephone a long hard stare, sighs, relents.

She reaches for the receiver, takes it in hand, and...

KABOOM?

NO!

Another hand's grasped onto hers, forcing the receiver to stay in the cradle.

"Jesus Christ Roger—"

"Keep your hands straight in the air. Don't say a word."

"What am I under arres—"

"Shhh! Please Simone..." He flips off the power bar on her desk. He reaches for the still-ringing phone, picking up the receiver. He looks himself over. No glow. He tears out the phone cord and stands Simmons up. "Stay absolutely quiet."

She's trusting but she wants answers. He pats her down a little. He finds nothing.

She grimaces.

"Have to go," he answers. "I'll explain la—"

"Simmons!" Burgess is walking briskly out her office, her cell phone in her right hand, waving it. "Tell me you're not stupid enough to give one of your ratbag sources my number! I got a guy on hold who—"

Jech puts a hand over Burgess' mouth, trying to grab her phone with his other. Burgess backs up, further enraged, phone still transmitting. She's about to recommence her shouting when...

"You owe me," Jerry says turning to Simmons. He's pointing at his computer monitor. "I have just started the official YouTube channel of one, Simone—"

POOF!

Jerry—silently, instantly—bursts into a cloud of reddish-pink dust. Headphones that were around his neck fall to his seat.

People who saw it act out of confused horror. Some panic. Others who weren't paying attention act out of plain confusion. Dust hovers in the air as Jech drags a catatonic Simmons past a trembling Burgess, toward the office door.

FIRES BURN, CARS ARE OVERTURNED. It's chaos. Crimson didn't go far, but he's nowhere to be seen now. Nand and The Professor stand under the theater marquee watching as EMS workers respond to the scene. They stare blankly. No output.

21

IF THEY CAN DO IT TO YOU, THEY CAN DO IT TO ANYONE...

We're in the Whitehouse now... *Oooh fancy*. But don't get your hopes up. Our tour begins and ends in a bunker several hundred feet beneath the actual structure. The President sits in a cozy enough looking office in the depths of the Whitehouse bowels. Three secret service agents stand unobtrusively off to the side. The President hits a button on an intercom at his desk.

"Get me *Homeland*."

"Right away Mr. President."

President turns to the agents, "Wanna know why we haven't smoked this Dawkitt fella out yet."

Secret service agents nod in encouragement.

"Now, what's takin' so long..." President reaches for the intercom when... All comms go dark.

SQUAWK!

Head of President's detail bursts into the bunker mid-action, "Post Eagle, entering nest." He immediately begins checking all tech in the room. President is about to speak when the agent interrupts him, "Mr. President we just received notice of a possible attack. We had to disable all of your comm equipment."

President tries to be stoic, "What's the situation son?"

"We'll have that information shortly Mr. President. In the meantime..." Head of detail directs his attention to the three agents. "Posts 3, 4, and 5, shut off receivers."

The agents do just that, almost in perfect simultaneity. The second they do though... *POP! POP! POP!* Their heads split open from various angles. Brains everywhere.

Head of detail reacts. "Room's not secure! We have to get you out of here Mr. President—"

POP!

Face of Head of Detail blows off. Brains and skull follow it. All gore lands on the President now alone in his bunker, covered in red pectin, shaking.

WE SEE FINGERS AT A keyboard and mouse. We whip around the fingers and up to reveal a screen showing pixelated representations of info-tech devices. Smartphones, laptops, *radio equipment...* We spin upward and outward to reveal that those fingers-typing belong to Crimson. Of course they do. He's sitting at the computer, a glow dissipating all around his head. A chandelier of SPAS-12 shotguns is suspended over him each gun aimed at a different forty-five-degree angle at his skull. Mechanical devices cover each and every trigger. Several barrels emit smoke.

THE FIVE INTERVENTIONISTS WATCH THE proscenium television. Signal's over-air broadcast unscrambled by bunny-ears. Bob Cross is addressing the public,

Tonight will be our final broadcast. We issue it with the best interests of the public in mind, knowing that even this broadcast, although essential, puts us all at risk.

Cross is shaking uncontrollably. His tremor affects his voice.

The w—world is in turmoil. Over a dozen more government officials have been assassinated in the past 24 hours and countless people around the world have been murdered, all seemingly at random. Authorities wish for us to remind you that victims were targeted through various information technologies. Those same authorities are urging the public to continue avoiding any and all behavior that may activate these technologies. E—even your voice could trigger an attack should you be near anything with a microphone. If you cannot communicate through pencil and paper, then please refrain. If you must speak, avoid common phrases, buzzwords, and names. Avoid travel, unless, if you have access to spaces off-grid, please seek them out and shelter there. If you haven't already, please destroy your phones, computers, and anything else that can send or receive information electronically. Power grids will remain off until further notice, power for the purposes of this broadcast notwithstanding, and police will continue confiscating any and all generators, batteries, automobiles, and other power sources. Government officials will be disseminating updated lists of all technologies known to have triggered attacks, as well as any further instructions for keeping you and your families safe. But p —please... Please please... Do not attempt to speak with these officials. Just take the information they give in the blue envelope provided. The envelope is displayed as follows:

Cross holds up a token envelope so home audiences will

understand. He's almost finished, but it's always darkest before the dawn of the sign-off...

Now, lastly, at the end of this sentence, please destroy your tele-visions.

Cross nods at the audience then sighs in relief. He looks off in the distance like he's seeking approval from someone. He nods again, gets up, still in shock. He quickly if aimlessly walks off camera.

The five heroes have watched with all due concern. Now Nand is to be the first to comment but he needs The Professor's permission to do so. He waits.

Professor waves an electronic device around the room. Satisfied, he grabs the plug of the television cord at the wall outlet. He's about to pull when...

PSSST! The test pattern pops away and a familiar malice comes back on the tube. Crimson's sitting in front of a wall of video monitors flashing various representations of various types of data. He's in address mode.

Not gonna mince any more words than the ones I'm currently usin'... This all ends, Amerika, when you turn your lives back on and plug your souls back in n' start letting me recommence with weedin' you out. Simple as this: you're a use to me, you live. You're not, you die. You're already turning those machines back on as we speak anyhow. Many a'ya never even turned 'em off. Look for yo'selves...

Crim gestures at the video monitors behind him. There's an eight-by-five bank of mostly blank screens. However, the leftmost of the top row is rapidly filling with icons we're meant to understand are devices coming online. First screen's filled completely now and the one next to it is already past two-thirds full.

Won't be long but why wait at all? You're a use to me, you live. You're not, you die. And! Take heed Amerika. Take heed of these next few words constitutive of my unending grace: there's nobody of more use to me right now than those of you who can truly see the greater cause, the greater good, who can truly embrace it, and who can truly and faithfully help they brothas and sistas who cannot yet see, to open they eyes. Who will hasten those brothas and sistas in gettin' turned back on and tuned back in for their day of reckoning. Show them the way. Help them achieve submission through transmission and you all will be of a value greater than The Word is to God! You're a use to me, you live. You're not, you die.

SMASH! The Professor puts a baseball bat through the television. He's following the orders of Bob Cross though that's clearly incidental. There's no catharsis for him in this but there is a pause to the dissonance. A pause barely any length of time at all yet next to eternity relative the circumstances. He uses the baseball bat to sweep the TV rubble off the proscenium. He looks up and nods at Nand, still waiting for that *ok* to speak. Nand proceeds.

"Crimson's forced our hand long before this. We had to act long before this therefore. We have to bring him into daylight now. Not just to stop him—to stop the people from becoming him trying to appease him."

Nothing but agreement from all.

IT'S ONLY BEEN A FEW days and it's already chaos. People have flooded into the streets of West Brandon searching desperately for any device that may transmit information, hoping to destroy it or worse force someone 'useless' to operate it. There's a police presence but there's no policing. There's just a subset of members of various sides with more weaponry and armor and badges than anyone else. It's a people divided into those hoping to appease Crim, those hoping to appease the powers-that-be, and those who refuse to abet the quick and brutal death Crimson intends or the slow and painful death our luddite masters don't even realize they're ensuring. Far fewer constitute this latter group.

How can we tell there are fewer? Why would these defiant ones even be out in the streets to make us privy to such facts? To flee of course. Crim appeasers and Fed appeasers have chased the defiant one's into the streets and are hunting them. Each neighborhood is either occupied by Crim disciples or Fed sycophants. Either mob's members march shoulder to shoulder in their respective neighborhoods, wearing sporting gear, duct tape, even extra layers of clothing for armor. Some wear cop gear... Probably because they're cops... All appeasers brandish unvarnished billy clubs. A crude beige beater someone whipped up as quickly as possible on a lathe somewhere. *Quick* so there's a club for every appeaser. *Quick* before the lathe's generator's confiscated.

Not all hunt. Some are smashing into storefronts of web service providers, phone companies, anywhere they believe the internet is 'held'. Others are tearing hoods off automobile's looking for batteries already removed by armed forces. Some kneel on the sidewalks in front of looted storefronts trying to connect wireless routers to AA batteries hoping to appease Crim. Others kneel, crushing those batteries with hammers and rocks hoping to appease nameless faceless bureaucrats everywhere. It's all chaos and desperation with a tremendous amount of stupidity thrown in too. Quick question: which of these three societal defects feed the others *and* in what proportion *and* in what order? Never mind...

AROUND A CORNER IN A blind alley three men accost a fourth. The fourth is much older. Two of the younger have pinned the elder against a wall, flanking him, hooking his arms and pushing hard against his shoulders. The third young man holds a knife to the elder's throat in one hand and a portable two-way radio in the other. He's jabbing the tip of the knife into the elder's throat just enough to leave a shaving nick's worth of blood each poke.

"Say it!" the kid shouts.

"Wh—why—" the old man shudders.

"For the greater good!"

"N—No... *Why* are you doing this?"

"For the greater good!"

"Who'll take care of your mo—"

"Say your fucking name!"

Old man is a defiant one for a reason. Despite his fear and confusion, "No son... Never."

"You're useless! I'll show *him* I'm not..." Son arcs the knife backward to plunge it into his dad's stomach. Sets it swinging toward the father like on a pendulum when...

BIM! BIM! BIM!

Young ones collapse. All three. Knife's in dirt *not* bowel but the old man doesn't look relieved at all. Why would he?

"You bastard! You killed my so—"

Jech puts a hand over the man's mouth, leans in. Doesn't hold the elder hard but censorship's achieved easy as guy's already against a wall.

"He's fine," Jech assures. "Look into his eyes. Don't say a word." He eases off, lets dad see. Reveals he's taken the man's wallet in the embrace yet dad don't care. Why would he? Jech flips open the section that holds the driver's license, eyeing it as he kneels to pick up the two-way radio. Grabs the son's wallet while he's down there.

Now he rises, steps clear. Readies the radio and says the father's name into the receiver... Nothing. He opens the son's wallet, reads the ID card, says the name into the re-

BOOOOM!

Glow bursts out of Jech's brow. The old man startles, then realizes. He hunkers down to his son, putting a hand to his forehead. Another realization now...

"You're the Masked—"

"I hate that name." He smashes the kid's two-way over his knee. "You've got five minutes to talk to your boy. He may not look it, but he can hear everything you're saying. Look into his eyes. Don't say his name. Make those minutes count."

Father doesn't even hesitate to console a son who just seconds ago was about to gut him. Why would he?

Jech moves to the entrance of the empty alley and stands firm between the family and the rioters. He's observing the chaos as he inserts an earbud of his own very special radio. He puts a finger to ear.

"Professor!"

SQUAWK! You transmitting?

Light on the receiver is blue. "Just to you."

Good.

"What the hell are we gonna do?"

Get to the lab Jech. The rest of us are making our way there now.

"Is Simone with you?"

Yes.

Deepest relief. "I'm ten minutes away. Be there in fifteen."

22

———

FINAL INTERVENTION

Lab Facility: Undisclosed Location.

All meet a last time before the intervention. Our five heroes are here, as is Suit-Man, a few dozen more feds, lot of soldiers. Professor and Nand flank a whiteboard looking out at everyone. Soldiers are seated. Feds stand behind them, looming. Minding them? Board's got a large circle at its center with FSA headquarters sketched inside. Far outside the circle, at 5 o'clock, is a square with 'COMM' written in it. *COMM* sits next to a little sticker of a rocket.

Everything is ready.

Lytrall will be the first to speak.

Everything is ready. Every one must be ready.

He steps away from the board. Moves sufficiently close to the soldiers. Close enough to take the whole of this platoon in. Attends to the men solemn. *Last lecture of your life Toll...*

"I hope you're scared," he begins. "I hope so. I hope you're scared because anything less means you may just have convinced yourselves salvation comes of appeasement.

Appeasement of Crim, sure, like so many out there in those streets have attempted, failed. Though maybe you intend appeasement of the corruption at your backs? Your heels?" He gestures to the Feds at the rear of the room.

The men twist in their chairs to eye the bureaucrats. To describe these soldiers' faces at all accurately would be to say they look unimpressed. It's the training but the bureaucrats don't know it. Suits take the apathy as assent, like this interventionist freak Lytrall's stirred in the men some judgement along the lines of: *these assholes don't farm*. Suit-Man and the rest are visibly affronted. Suit's about to challenge The Professor when...

"Shut that little tyrant mouth of yours y' luddite worm!"

Nand's moved shoulder to shoulder with Lytrall. Soldiers burst up in salute at him. He returns gesture. Men turn to face the bureaucrats. This isn't their training. They're stone like their superior officer. The Business hits Suit-Man with an intensity that shuts his slack bureaucrat jaw up near instantly only not before the anger conveyed in his desperate gaping maw turns to shock then fear then cowardice.

Lytrall nods appreciatively at all-who've-stepped-in as all-who've-stepped-in return to their marks.

Room settles.

He recommences.

"I hope you're scared because that means you've yet to convince yourselves appeasement brings peace *not just* delusion then death. You stand up to the force at your heels so stoic. You look so stoic but you better be *scared to death* under all that dispassion. You know how hastily this plan has been put together. Put together to stop a trickster who's managed to not just take from you when you give but take from you when you take. A force that can turn you to dust for your words. For the names of those dearest to you. Your children. For your *I love yous*. A force only ever accelerated by opposition.

"I speak of *hope* in your fears though I understand if for you all hope is lost... Though I need you scared not hopeless. Ah, but any reasonable man *will* be hopeless! So here's what you will do. You will tear into that hopelessness. Dig! Find the solace that you *the reasonable* know such a hopelessness must give. You've lost all hope because you're going to die. You know the solace in this. Don't deprive yourself of it. Say it.

Your death will free you from him.

"Oh, but he will not give you this satisfaction! *Freedom from Crimson Dawkitt?*" He scoffs. "Death is not coming for you, therefore. He will not give you *that* satisfaction. He will never give you such, but not dying today guarantees you a tomorrow. Knowledge of a tomorrow brings hope... He will not give you this satisfaction either. He needs you hopeless not scared.

"He can't let you live. He can't let you die.

"Your living torments him. Your dying torments him.

"That may be all that torments him in this world though it means a world of endless torment. A man in such a state is never formidable. He's pitiable. We do not defeat the pitiable. The pitiable are already defeated. We simply dispose of their remains."

The soldiers react to these words as though their eulogy. They don't look motivated. They look scared. Good.

"Mr. Nand."

Nand gets right into it. He points to the large hoop on the board. "Alright, this is our threat circle. Cross this line and Jane, his men, even Crimson may engage you. Command center will be here..." He circles the square with 'COMM' written in it. "...And Icarus here." He circles the rocket. "Now, this can't be stressed enough, no one but The Professor and Jech are to use IT. We don't want anyone setting off one of Crimson's suiciders."

A CANVASSED PERSONNEL TRUCK BARRELS down a four-lane pass to the east checkpoint of FSA headquarters. We hear Nand's voice narrating the offensive.

Phase one: transport breaches here...

The personnel truck swerves outside and around the checkpoint barrier. Truck's too big to clear the terminals. The four mercs manning the gate dive out of the way. Truck picks up speed as the guards regroup and pack into an armed assault vehicle at the ready, attempting to give chase.

...Trees should provide decent cover.

Truck moves up the twisting lanes flanked on both sides by dense forest.

...then it's a straight shot to FSA Plaza.

Gunners shoot at the truck now at maximal speed. Truck charges on, blasting through the plaza barricades as more hired-guns dive out of the way.

...After Alpha Team has breached, they thin out Jane's men
opening the door for Jech. Phase one complete!

. . .

TURRET MINI GUNNERS SHRED THE transport truck to pieces from up high. Blood and guts fly from all sections of the truck lacking armor. Not a single soldier has made it out.

On the ground, ten mercs sparsely distributed about twenty yards from the rear of the truck fire carbine rounds. Job of the ten is to shoot anywhere a transport occupant might poke a gun out. Or anything more fleshy...

The gunfire continues for fun and profit. A half-minute for the mercs to be mercenaries another half-minute for the mercs to be the Jane Brand sadists they are. Which one's for fun and which one's for profit? Pros ease off their triggers now as the truck stands looking like hammered headcheese in a camo gravy boat.

A leader-looking merc makes chopping motions at the vehicle. Three lackeys move out from behind *Merc-Leader*. Approach the truck with caution when...

BANG! BANG!

Muzzle flair can be seen from an opening at the rear of the troop carrier. Investigating mercs roll clear and start firing back. *Merc-1* catches sight of an M16 barrel sneaking out of a hole in the canvas. He fires in its direction. M16 adjusts its angle. It fires and Merc-1 goes down. *Merc-2* and *Merc-3* fall back and let the turret gunners fire anew. M16 pokes out from canvas shooting at one of the mini-gunners. Gunner shreds what's left of the canvas where the barrel protrudes but it's the M16 that takes out the turret gunner!

It was a one-in-a-million shot and the soldier in the carrier isn't finished. He's about to do it again. Barrel protrudes from opposite side of the canvas. *BOOM!* Shot takes out the other gunner too!

All is silence. Troop carrier sits in tatters. Hired-guns to its rear look on in disbelief when...

Truck-Soldier slinks out the side of the transport box and moves around to the front, out of sight. All *Trucker*'s attackers can discern is that he's covered in head to toe with tac gear. Not a bit of daylight hitting him. That don't make him invincible though...

More chopping from Merc-Leader as Merc-2 and Merc-3 take up positions at the driver's side and the rear respectively. Merc-3 fires a couple shots along the passenger side as Merc-2 rushes to the front.

Trucker is shooting back in the direction of Merc-3 when he's hit in his left shoulder by Merc-2. Trucker spins to fire. Merc 2 goes down! When's this guy's luck going to run out? He hunkers with his back to the transport's steaming radiator now. He's catching his breath. *Time to go after Merc-3.* He turns to face the grill and sidles to its edge. His balaclava'd face inches out from that edge stopping just before its right eye comes into view. Then...

"Drop the gun!" is heard from behind Trucker! Remaining pros must have snuck from around the rear carrier and positioned themselves at its front. Got the drop on truck-soldier while his back was turned.

We can't see much of Trucker's expression, but we can certainly see his eye narrowing as he stealthily swaps out the spent clip of his M16 for a fresh one. He's gonna push his luck as far as it will take him. He spins around ready to take on the eight remaining gunners when...

Luck's run out.

He spins only to meet at least two dozen freshly arrived men led by Jane himself. We can't see his face, but Trucker must look smashed by a ton of bricks. He's going out guns blazing though!

BOOM! BOOM! BOOM! BOOM!
En masse, the pros return fire.
BOOM! BOOM! BOOM! BOOM!
Trucker's getting hit all over. Brought to his knees but he's still firing... And hitting everything he aims at! It's almost like he's got a vendetta or something cuz he's taking down any merc who hits 'em the second that merc hits 'em. The super soldier can't take much more though. He's prone yet still squirming, trying to get to cover that isn't there.

Jane knows it's over. "Cease fire!"

He sets out walking toward the writhing miracle. On the way he takes out his pack of smokes and cuts a third of a filter off one. It's lit by the time he gets to the man now more wound than warrior.

Trucker rolls to his side, tries raising the M16 but Jane just kicks it away. Merc then crouches to get a better look at what he's amazed ain't death. Cigarette dangles from mouth. He pulls out his 410 and puts it to Truck's forehead.

Trucker decides there's nothing left to do but condescend his executioner. He speaks in a strained hush. "Don't you think you should check the safety's not on asshole?"

Jane smirks. "Pulling the trigger oughtta confirm that..."

Smirk fades.

BANG!

It's over.

Jane's down...

Jane's down?

Trucker lurches upward firing bottle fly Glocks. *BIM! BIM! BIM!* Scratch three more pros!

"Try and find a hole in that armor boys!" shouts Merc-4.

Jane's men return fire. Each hit to Trucker sends the man who shot him to the ground, convulsing. Truck continues with the Dual Glock Shock as he inches closer and closer back to the transport. Twelve more men are down by the time he gets to the passenger side.

Mercenaries not already on the scene start pouring out of the FSA buildings.

Truck grabs the bottle fly Colt out the cab. Starts taking out gunners furthest away while those closer take themselves out shooting him. One decides to toss a grenade. *BOOM!* Trucker's blown back against the side of the transport as Grenade-Merc flies at the opposing angle right through five allies. Topples them like bowling pins.

Up and back in it, Trucker's firing the PSG1. He takes out two more men heading for the turret stations. Then...

POOSH!

Merc-3 nets him from a standing position on top of the cab. Forgot about him.

Merc-Leader sees this, rocks a fist in the air grinning a grin that looks like a shit won't come but he'll be damned if it's gonna ruin his birthday. Shouts, "Cease fire!"

Merc-3 jumps off the truck as Leader points to him and two others. "You three with me. Everyone else fall back!"

All hop to action. *Somebody grab Jane!* Leader, Merc-3, and Merc-4 stand on Trucker's netting keeping him pinned. Merc-5 takes the PSG1 out from under our net-bound Trucker.

He holds it up. "Light," he says, nodding.

Leader focuses on something else. "Let's get a look at this guy's armor."

Cautiously, Merc-5 lets Trucker's head poke through the netting. *What other tricks might he have up his sleeve?* Merc-Leader knocks off the helmet then pulls off the balaclava. Turns it inside out in the process. Marvels at the green bulletproof paneling he's slipped out of the lining. Shows Merc-3 the micro-porous material on the one side of it. Pores flicker with the electric arc of residual plasma. More grinning. "Crimson's going to be so happy when he sees what we brung him."

Trucker was Jech all along! Surprised?

Jech just stares a million miles through Merc-Leader. It's not some tough guy act though. He's looking at what's coming up behind.

SWOOSH!

Etty and one of The Professor's mechanical men fly in from out of nowhere and start clobbering Jane's men. Jech begins twisting his way out of the netting. Etty fights like fluid but with Nand's ability to anticipate incoming attacks. *SPLISH! SPLASH! SPLISH!* and the pros go flying. Mech-Man fights smooth too though encumbered by a large cable wired into the back of his head.

SIMMONS CONTROLS THE MECHANICAL MAN via something like a PlayStation controller. The controller's wired to a Command Center terminal. Terminal features a monitor with an interface like a third-person action game.

"How do you like it?" Professor asks, taking a second to look away from his binoculars.

"It's no Leisure Suit Larry..." she cracks.

"And you guys think my code words are obscure..." Nand scoffs.

TWO OF FOUR MERCS ARE down and *WHAM!* Etty adds a third with a spin kick. Man and mech continue to go round and round with the last remaining pro as two snipers scramble across the roof of FSA headquarters. They're in position and taking aim at our fighters when... *BIM! BIM!* Jech, free the netting, takes the snipers out with the PSG1. He walks over to Merc-Leader and casually baps him one with his plasma glove. Leader's down. They're all down.

Phase one complete.

Jech nods at Etty, impressed. "Three and a half."

Etty grins, holds up some fingers. *Four!*

"Had help." Jech puts a hand on the mech's shoulder. Mechanical man reaches out and hugs him. Wasn't expecting this... Hero turns to Etty for an explanation. Etty shrugs. Mech rests his head over Jech's heart now, right palm caressing his midsection.

SIMMONS TURNS to The Professor with a wry smile. Prof shakes his head, tongue protruding in cheek pocket.

HE PRIES OFF THE MECHANICAL man. "Ok fella, save it for the victory party." Focuses on Etty again. "Time to clean this up." He's gesturing all around. "I'll clear what's left outta there." Gesture settles into a point pointing at FSA headquarters.

Etty nods, runs back toward Command. Mechanical Man gives Jech a kiss on the cheek and runs back in that direction too. He's looping up cable as he goes.

Something catches the interventionist's eye. It's Jane's 410. He picks it up, examines it a second, breaks it over his knee.

THE PROFESSOR'S WATCHING SOME MONITORS tapped into FSA security. Sees Jech approaching FSA's front door. "Looks like he's in Mr. Nand. Let's hope Crimson's home."

No response.

"Mr. Nand?" He glances away from the terminal.

No Nand.

NAND'S SLIPPED AWAY TO STALK the main headquarters. Looking for Jane. He's entered a large server room. The room's just row upon row of cabinets glowing like chunky refrigerator-shaped Christmas trees. Speaking of refrigerators, the rooms cold. Not *can see your breath cold,* yet chew on a fried perogy a second or two and you'll be huffing a plume for a time. The government likes to keep their secrets nice and chilled it seems.

On Nand stalks...

But who's stalking who? Turns out Jane's gotten the drop on him. Traitor's slinking along some server racks hugging them, crouched, holding a newly acquired .45. He creeps up to the corner of the last cabinet and peeks around. He's just in time to see Nand turn a similar corner up ahead at the end of the row. If we were looking down on these guys it would come off like a game of Pac-Man.

On Jane stalks...

He's moving a little more briskly up to where he saw Nand last. He's just abou—

He hasn't gotten the drop on anyone!

Nand snags Jane around the neck with a noose of ethernet cables. He's poked the noose through an empty server slot of the cabinet between them.

CRUNCH!

Wrenches Jane's head into that cabinet. He lets him have a little slack and...

CRUNCH!

Does it again.

Jane's dazed to hell. Nand pivots around the cabinet corner to face him. Eyes the woozy Judas up and down and *CRUNCH!* Whomps his head into the cabinet one more time for good measure, disarms him in the process as he has time again, putting the .45 in his belt. He grabs the end of the Ethernet noose and drags Jane into the periphery of the massive server room. He slingshot whips him around to his front, letting go of the noose just in time to send turncoat flying halfway across the space. Server room periphery alone is gymnasium-width so that's quite the flight...

Jane struggles to get to his feet, his bell still a lot rung. Sees Nand bearing down on him. He scoffs at the approaching soldier, "You're not gonna kill me. Don't even kid yourself."

"I'm taking you in," Nand pounds.

"Where? Gonna have me court-martialed? I'm *for-profit* old man." Jane's finally back on his feet but wobbly. "You making a citizen's arrest?"

Nand shakes his head. "I'm dropping you in a lockbox and lettin' the families of my men have the key."

Jane doesn't like the sound of this. Tries for stoic nonetheless. "You're gonna have to work for it."

"Be a first..."

Then...

Nand, fast as a piston at full bore, lets go with three straight rights. *CRUNCH! CRACK! CRUNCH!* Nose, teeth, nose, and Jane's on his ass again spittin' teeth through flowing nostril blood. Spittin' as cuffs are slipped on. Slipped on a busted man barely noticing through those tear-filled eyes.

Nand still looks like he wants to take Jane to pieces. *Leave it to the adjudicators? Abide the principle?* He crouches. Lifts Jane's head by the hair in order that the traitor see his conviction. "Enjoy these few seconds I give you to sit in your pain. Things will never be this good for you again."

Jane breathes wheezily through crooked nose and toothless maw. Makes a last appeal. "Sthurely you won't mind me cauthing a little more damage to mythelf then? How 'bout a lathst thigarette?" He tilts his head at the pack of Marlboros in his breast pocket.

"Nice try." Nand wrenches him to his feet.

"No lastht requesthts? Am I not a man condemned?"

"Fine," soldier says begrudgingly.

Jane greedily takes his cigarettes out of his pocket. "Ha! That thense of honor of yourth. Getsth you every time..."

"Just light one."

He fumbles with the pack. His cuffed hands make it difficult to get a smoke out.

Nand gets fed up with this fast. He moves to Jane to take him into custody. "Alright. You had your chance."

Seamless, Jane goes from fumbling to deft. He drives the pack of cigarettes up and into Nand's face. Soldier stumbles backward as the pack falls off his chin revealing manicure scissors stuck firmly in jaw. He reflexively rips them out.

Jane's taken back his .45 in the fracas. He holds it in cuffed hands at Nand's chest. Nand's perfectly still, not breaking eye contact. Jane gloats. "Crimsthon taught me a few thingths about not telegraphing my movesth."

Nand's stone.

"Any lathst wordths?"

Eyes narrow. "You sound ridiculou—"

BANG! BANG! BANG! Jane angrily drives three bullets into his mentor's chest.

Nand tries to retain his usual stone-faced demeanor despite the fatal wounds. He can't manage it however. His face contorts to a look of slight pain but also, incongruously, a look of disappointment.

Then...

Jane collapses, dead...

Jane?

He has three bullet holes in his chest.

Soldier pulls that plate of The Professor's bulletproof teflon out from his shirt. Tosses it onto Jane's corpse. He turns, walks away.

NAND'S WALKING OUT THE FRONT door of FSA headquarters as Jech sidles up to him dragging two pros.

"Jane?"

Shakes his head. Jech comprehends.

"Crimson?"

Interventionist shakes his head right back. "If he's in there, he's hiding like a cockroach."

"*Final Phase: Information Warfare?*"

"Yeah," says Jech. "Take these."

Nand nods, starts dragging the two mercs back to where The Professor, Simmons, and Etty wait for further orders. He joins some Soldiers detaining what's gotta be the last remaining hired guns half-free and they all recede into the distance.

THE FEDERAL SECURITY AGENCY OF Amerika building stands hubristic. Like the shiny glass file cabinet full of all our surreptitiously gleaned privacy that it is.

SQUAWK! It's The Professor's voice on the box.

Ready?

Jech pushes a button on an earpiece. "Ready."
PA loudspeaker blares out across the compound,

Clear ring of operation. Bunker buster in 120 seconds.

Jech takes out a fob much like The Professor's but with just a single button on it. He waits.

THE PROFESSOR, SIMMONS, ETTY, AND Nand stand at the makeshift command center. They wait.

BACK TO JECH NOW. STILL waiting. Hasn't moved an inch. *SQUAWK!*

Bunker buster in 10, 9, 8...

An old B-17 bomber comes chugging into view.

...2, 1, buster is a go.

The B-17 roars past the top of the complex releasing a large missile from under its left wing. Missile pierces into the building with an anticlimactic thud. *Seemingly* anticlimactic... Jech hits the button on his fob and the complex erupts in smoke, dust, and debris from out its center. Sides crumble inward.

FSA is trash.

23

CLEAN UP

The feds have begun excavating the rubble but not before a little paperwork of course. Jech and The Professor are granted a limited presence. *Limited* because the feds haven't found Crimson yet. *Limited* because why let the experts complete the task when you can have elected officials and the bureaucrats who love them polish the frame to sign the canvas?

"They know to stop the second they see that glow?"

"Couldn't have been clearer," Professor answers. He eyes Jech a little suspiciously. Jech catches this.

"What?"

Eyes narrow, "Any glow on *you* after you blew the place?"

Oh crap... "I wasn't paying attention."

"You need to be more caref—"

SQUAWK!

Midas on your six.

Pair spins one-eighty. It's a glow in the distance across a freeway, in a football field of a military academy. Jech looks down the PSG1 scope. Surprise surprise. It's Crimson, holding a walkie in one hand, batting at himself with the other. Glow.

He's waving a Jech over who's already bursting toward.

THEY FACE EACH OTHER FROM opposing end zones. Jech removes his jacket and Colt, drops them, sets out walking. Crim mirrors this step for step. Is he being led here? Led by Jech? Or, is the only time Crim'll meet a man half way when it's to keep that man from going a single step further?

They stop ten yards apart, Jech cautious, Crim *blasé*.

May be *blasé* but that won't stop him from taunting. "Once ya submit to me, world follows."

Vigilante turns as cold as Crim at this hubris. "And what if the world turns its back?" Eyes of the nemesis narrow near imperceptibly. Is this curiosity for him? "World doesn't have to face you to stop you," Jech insists. "The world just has to stay home. They give you nothing, you have nothing."

"Then I take it."

"Then they make sure there's nothing to take. Easiest thing in the world to have nothing. Even easier when you're *having nothing* for a cause."

"Then I—"

"No!" Jech growls. "*No. You. Won't.* The world turns its back on you, your empire crumbles. You need them more than they need you... *Can you farm?*"

Crim's stone.

"Didn't think so," Jech scoffs. "*The bandit who reaps the whole of the other's harvest today next year only reaps the winter.* I don't know what you think great power is, but last time I checked it didn't involve complete and utter dependence on *the people* to make the world happen for you. You know what I think? I think I'm looking at just another pathetic old man only good for flippin' dead switches only he can't even find a switch to flip." He points in the direction of the FSA rubble. "You have lost all control. And you never had *the pow'r*."

Crimson is as taken aback by this mockery as a person of his disposition can be. Jech's rebuke changes him like a drip from a glacier changes the glacier. But a change is a change.

Villain opens his arms, inviting Jech. "All right *La Boetie*, let's put that theory to the test."

And with that, the battle commences.

THEY CHARGE TOWARD EACH OTHER, colliding like they're on a field of battle. Because they are. They're clobbering each other with complete abandon. They go back and forth, back and forth, punching, kicking, kneeing, chopping, gouging... Each attack landing and creating a glow on the attacked that feeds back to the attacker. No blocking, no evasion, just short-range offense. Their blows continue as the glow intensifies and intensifies much more...

A solid glowing orb is amassing around them, engulfing them. Its diameter extends outward, rate of expansion increasing exponentially. The combatants' abuse continues too in perfect reciprocity as the diameter reaches twice the length of the football field.

THE WHOLE OF THE ACADEMY is a great solid sphere of gold.

INSIDE THAT SPHERE, AMIDST THE blonde fog, the battle continues. *Back, forth, back, forth, back, forth...* Crim hammers

Jech. Jech hammers Crim. Then... Crim breaks pattern. He inches to the left letting Jech take a swing right past him, stumbling him. *Be more careful!* He grabs Jech by the back of the neck and forces him into a hunch. Could almost weep at the vulnerability born of this contrived curvature... He commences pulverizing the hero's midsection with uppercuts. Uppers are fast as lightning too. He's digging through Jech's upper-body with his left hand like he's trying to break through and shake hands with his right.

Jech crumbles to Crim's rhythm. Time to puke glow and die? It's like that but he's still figuring things out. He gets the stochastic pattern. Grabs Crim's jackhammer of a wrist with both hands like he's Beowulf all over again! Crim struggles. It's futile. Jech rises up, digs deepest into that appendage and yanks. Lets go! Crim lurches just past as vigilante spins to catch him round the neck. *Put him to sleep Jech!*

No good. Crim's figuring faster. Crim's doing everything faster. He takes Jech's right hand in a crushing grip of his own. Separates it from its hold on his crown and lets loose with some head-butts. *SMASH! SMASH! SMASH!* he goes, the back of his head caving in his opponent's front. Takes Jech into a daze though can't quite get out of the sleeper. Wastes no time. Hops upward resting the dorsa of his feet in the pits of Jech's knees. Suspended, he twists his toes down and inside his dance partner's calves. He pries at them as he goes.

Sufficiently leveraged, he splits those legs like a wishbone. Holds 'em open. The two remain hopelessly intwined a second, then... Crim thrusts his torso back and kicks his feet forward. Rips Jech's legs right out from under him.

They topple backward.

SMASH! SMASH! SMASH! Crim's resumed the head-butts... *SMASH! SMASH!* ...Then rolls away.

Jech pulls the back of his skull out of the indentation it's made in the sod. Both fighters get to their feet. They face each other in slight repose. Crim takes out a knife. Who knows where he got it. He holds it in his right hand. Jech looks at him with a *what are you up to?* expression. Crimson waves the knife around like he's half taunting, half trying to confuse. Then, *apropos* of nothin', he grabs the blade with his left hand and rips it right out again, cutting deep. He opens his palm into opponent's face. Immense glow!

Jech's blinded, stumbling all over again!

Crim pounces. Jumps and clings onto Jech knocking him backward. Riding him down like a lumberjack riding a felled tree. Straddling his chest, he raises his knife and commences to plunging the blade into the hero's eyes. *IN/OUT, IN/OUT, IN/OUT, LEFT-EYE/RIGHT-EYE, LEFT-EYE/RIGHT-EYE...* Crim's eyes are bursting more light than Jech's. More and more as he stabs.

He'll keep Jech blind for as long as he wishes. *LEFT/RIGHT LEFT/RIGHT...* Then...

He's off him. Gone.

Eyes are repairing if slowly. Jech's only able to listen and feel just now. Glow beams eerily from eye sockets. He wanders. Looks to be listening with his outstretched hands as he moves. Everything is a silent blind, when...

SPLAT!

Crimson's driven the Colt right through Jech's back and two thirds out his chest. Keeps pushing on the gun only now at an angle, like a lever, forcing Jech to a kneeling position. He leaves his right hand firm on the butt of the Colt and uses his left to depress the switch transforming it into the PSG1. Gun extends deep into the sod. Jech's pinned, can't move, though that doesn't stop him from trying. Glow emits from both men's upper-bodies.

Crim walks literal circles around our man impaled. "*Smartah, fastah, bettah.*" Another pass and he stops. Reaches for Jech's waist. Pats him down a little. Jech tries to twist and turn away but he's preserved Lepidoptera now. Crim just pulls his torso to his right knee as a brace and holds him, immobilizes him a moment, continues the pat down. Finds what he's searching for in a cargo pant pocket. He releases the brace and circles back.

He examines Jech's eyes. They're repaired just fine. He dangles wrist and ankle restraints. Makes them dance a *jingle jangle.* "Looks like I found myself a switch." Jech responds with more twists and jerks. Tries but Crim's already got the man's arms up behind back as rifle abides the angle: keeps him propped at forty-five-degrees. Crim cuffs hands then kneels to apply the leg restraints.

Hero goes still butfor those hands. He's finagling. He's up to something. Real careful about what he's doing. Careful as a matter of precision, careful as a matter of secrecy. Because... The compressed air canister drops out the sleeve of his shirt. Can feel Crim still working on his left ankle so he finagles more. He gets the can in right hand, spinning it, index finger feeling for the groove of the actuator. Found it! *Spray* mode! He tickles the chain of the cuffs with his left hand, fingers as eyes for the canister held in his right. He feels his way to a link as good as any and guides the nozzle to within a millimeter of it. He depresses the nozzle and...

Crim snags it! Must have popped up behind faster than Jech could sense.

"What have we here?" Gives the object a once-over. "Ah, I see. Explains ya calm there brotha." Twirls the canister like a li'l baton a second then holds it a beat. Resolve? "Ah hell," he relents. "I don't want to deprive ya' of ya' toys..." He stuffs the canister into Jech's front hip pocket. A pocket as good as a million miles from those hands behind back. "Have at it *jewn-yah*."

Jech doesn't struggle for the air. Crim's onto him and this epistemic upper-hand didn't start with the failed cryogenics. He goes limp. The rifle will abide the angle anyway. He's tired. He rests.

"Right to pack it in little brotha..." Crim's about finished applying the shackles. "Best to get to planning any case for ya use. Done heard ya make for real good compost—"

A weak guttural,

D... nt...

"Huh?"

Do... t...

Don... t...

Curious, Crimson leans in to try to make out the chatter. "What was that?"

Jech responds weakly, *"Don't let him see your pain."*

"Wha—"

DON'T LET HIM SEE YOUR PAIN!

He raises his head as high as his angle will allow and lets out a huge howl in Crim's direction. He tenses up, shaking. Eyes close. Tremors intensify. The glow surrounding him begins to creep back into his chest and shoulder. Sympathy glow on Crimson's chest dissipates as well. It runs off and into Jech. Villain sees what's happening too late. He bolts up and backs away, wobbles a step as he goes.

All glow has crept into Jech now. It's all his. Tremor has stopped. He's absolutely still. Crim's head cocks at this. When...

KABOOM!

Pair fly away at opposite angles to each other. Jech flies in the direction the PSG1 determined. Up, back, and gone.

. . .

CRIMSON STUMBLES TOWARD THE CRATER made by the Jech bomb, dust settling all around it. The debris has cleared just enough for him to observe something curious through the blonde. What he beholds is Jech, standing, distant, glowing, eyes slate. *Don't think, don't feel, just move...*

SURPRISE!

A woman emerges from behind him. She's glowing too and naked as the day she divided Jech in two and manifested as his other half. She watches her counterpart, attempting to do everything he does. Speaking of what Jech does...

He extends his left arm revealing he's freed himself of the restraints in the kaboom. He opens his hand a little and the ankle cuffs tumble away from the wrist cuffs. He moves toward Crim, whipping the shackles around like a manriki as he goes. *Left to right, right to left, left left, right right*, then no discernible pattern. He increases the speed with which he spins and whips those shackles as he nears.

Crim watches trying to track the pattern. Gets distracted by *The Woman* a second. Any threat? Then back to the shackles. No rhythm alright. Some of the slate-death drains out of his eyes. A hint of fear displaces. Just a hint.

Jech's at full sprint now, chains whipping. The Woman charges alongside him. Triumphant.

BACK TO THE FOUR AT Command still watching *better* waiting for something, anything, to happen outside the golden sphere. They're rapt if powerless to know what's going on in there. Then...

A rumble.

The sphere expands as the rumble intensifies.

Rumble starts to die ratcheting all the way to stillness... It's a couple seconds of calm. Then... Sphere contracts to original size in an instant. From here it shrinks *only* slower and slower. Shrinks... Shrinks some more... *Is it dying?* It's contracted to singularity. *Is it over?*

Not quite.

POOOOM! It bursts outward but it's not growing. It's fragmenting in all directions, sending a shockwave toward our quartet of interventionists. Blows by them, mussing hair, leaving a sparkling golden residue on skin.

Behind our interventionists, behind all the wrecked coifs and gold dust, there's a reveal. We see Jane's army detained. We see feds, Suit-Man, soldiers that were never in any transport. We see a huge rocket, launchpad and all.

We turn back to see that the golden fragmentation has brought with it our combatants. Two stand, one kneels. Jech holds the scruff of the kneeling, shackled, Crimson's neck. The Woman watches her counterpart, awed. Jech hoists Crim up and hauls him toward Command. Prisoner shuffles quickly.

The crowd erupts!

Even some of Jane's men look relieved at the sight of a shackled Crim.

They march straight on by everyone. "Takin' out the trash here boss!" Jech says to The Professor.

"Yeah, take it out there," is the response.

Just one hand on Crim's shackles now. He reaches out and takes Simmons' in his free hand as he passes. She squeezes. There's caress all the way up to fingers separating.

She smiles a wistful smile a moment, then... Something catches her attention. Gingerly, she puts an arm out and stops The Woman prepared to follow Jech to the end. The two stare at each other confusedly. Simmons *ahems* in The Professor's direction, catching his attention. He waves a hand suggesting *it's fine, I'll explain later.*

Jech moves on, shuffling Crim to the rocket. He opens the elevator door of the crane adjacent the rocket and shoves the captive in. Door closes on the two as they rise.

THE ELEVATOR DOOR SLIDES OPEN and Jech's walking Crimson again. They move along a catwalk. At the other end of walk is a small shuttlecraft with an open door. Inside the craft is a containment unit, its door open too. Pair continues moving toward it.

Crim's eying that containment unit with cold interest. "Got any Tums on ya brotha?"

Jech ignores this.

"Come on now. Pepto Bismol? Anything?"

Nothing.

"Well that's rude." Crim halts.

Jech pivots to front, holds the shackles up to the convict's face. Holds onto them a lot tighter too. "Don't make me drag you."

"Just plain rude. Now, 'bout my indigestion..." Crim's mouth looks like it's attempting a smile. Face contorts slowly, deliberately. Baring his teeth at Jech we see it's another one of *those* smiles... *CHOMP! CHOMP!* He's gnashed those teeth once more.

FLASH. FLASH.

Then...

BEEP. BEEP. BEEP. BEEP.

"No!" Jech rips open Crim's coat. No bomb vest. Of course there isn't. He would have noticed it in battle.

Crim stares blankly. "I think somethin' I ate is disagreeing with me."

While Jech tries to figure, now's as good a time as any to take a trip down Crim's throat, right past that flashing tooth, past the uvula, over the vocal cords, esophagus, and right on into his stomach. Down there's a wad of C4 sitting in his gut like the most volatile fiber supplement anyone's ever seen, slight glow where it rests. Detonator LED flashes... Flashes...

What's Jech figured on the outside? No output.

KABOOM!

Explosion sends Jech sliding all the way down the catwalk smashing into the elevator door. Explosion sends Crim everywhere else. Glow.

GIVE JECH A MINUTE. HE'S crumpled but he'll burst out of it quick enough. We've all seen this before. There he goes. He rises. He'd collect himself but there's no time. He's looking down the opposite end of the catwalk. Nothing. Just containment unit and shuttle. Moves toward them cautious.

Approaches...

No amount of caution in the world...

SWOOSH!

Crim's swung up from the underside of the catwalk. The momentum's sent him up over and right down behind Jech. He lands with the chains of his broken restraints in hands, wrapping them around brotha's neck three times fast. Brotha grabs at them but can't do a thing. In one fluid motion, Crim's turned his back against Jech and's wrenched the chains over his shoulder. Pulls Jech off his feet, neck first, spinning. Spins a mite more and lets go sling-shotting him into the containment unit. Door slams.

There's struggling and shouting from inside the

container. It's all silence on the other side. Professor-Tech is soundproof *for all your interventionist storing convenience.* Crim puts his face to the glass looking intently at his captive.

He's only enjoying this... Jech stops the shouting. He matches Crim's expression, refusing him any more satisfaction.

Crim's agitated by this, sure. Behavioristically indifferent of course. He puts his face closer to the glass and huffs a little fog onto it. He draws a frown over Jech's blank expression.

"That's better."

DING!

Our villain backs away from the containment unit now *containing* only a Jech-sicle. Crim closes the shuttle craft door and the launch sequence initiates automatically.

We hear a disembodied mechanical voice, "Launch sequence initiated. Launching shuttle in 10, 9, 8..."

He continues backing away.

"3, 2, 1, ignition."

ROAR! The rocket's rumble can be felt as its shuttle begins to rise parallel to Crimson. Rocket moves faster and faster as it climbs. He opens his arms at the engine blast. If not for his stale visage, you'd swear he was basking in the heat and flame.

ROOOOOAAAAAAARRRRRRRRR! Then...

Stillness, silence. The rocket is gone.

Jech is gone.

24

SPACE MAN

Crimson heads back to the elevator, his mouth cracking the slightest of smiles. Genuine too. He pushes the call button. The door opens. He pauses. Hint-smile vanishes.

He's staring at a brick wall. A literal brick wall. He lashes out, throwing a punch. *SMACK!* What did he expect? It's a brick wall. It just stands there with all the intact integrity of a brick wall. What about that call button? He's already pushing the hell out of it again, over and over. No good. He's back to pounding. *THUD! THUD! THUD! THUD! THUD!* ... Then...

"Off."

The wall disintegrates into pixels. Did Crim do this? Pixels evaporate into digital dust. Everything else around him does the same. He's standing in grey slate with yellow grid running all around it. He's looking for the door.

"Locked in. And outta tricks," Jech says walking toward. Locked into a new Black Hole, evidently...

Crimson charges.

"Crimson bound."

Digital chains amass around the villain slowing him to a crawl then a stop. Just Crim's head is *unbound*, poking through the chains. He kneels before Jech.

"Off!" Crim tries.

Nothing.

"Only me." Jech raises his eyebrows a couple times at the helpless captive. He's going to bat that mouse around a little. "Grandpa Crimson!" he requests.

A backyard materializes around the pair. Children are playing happily while adults prepare food on a grill and picnic tables. A Father-Looking person manning the grill notices Crimson.

"Hey everybody, let's get a picture with grandpa!"

The children surround Crim hugging on him as the father readies the camera.

"Aw come on, give grandpa a kiss."

Two little kids lean in and kiss Crim on the cheeks like it's a Norman Rockwell painting. *CLICK!* He ignores the familial bullshit but looks at Jech with what you would almost swear is imploring.

"Puppies for grandpa Crimson," Jech retorts.

A dozen or so puppies join the grandkids in the merriment. Crim remains passive though he stares with that same hint of imploring. Stares as the puppies lick at his face and the children hug and squeeze. Then...

"I'm gonna get outta here someday..." he insists.

"Oh, you're gonna get out of here in about fifteen minutes Grandpa Crim." Jech grins. "You're a learned man so let me ask ya, how long does it take a ray of light to escape the sun's core?"

Crimson doesn't bite.

"Not gonna play? Fine. The answer is: a million years! Light rays! Made of photons! Tiny little particles that move at the speed of... You guessed it! *Light!* It takes them a million years to escape the gravity of the sun's core." he affects a quizzical tone. "How long do you think it would take *you*?"

No change in Crim's demeanor. But... "Naw."

"What's that?"

"Naw. You're not gonna take me outta here t' put me inna real rocket."

"Naw?"

"Naw."

"Well guess what? We've been outside of Earth's orbit for over an hour now."

"Impossible. Time don't pass outside a' here."

"That was a feature not a bug. Doesn't come standard either."

"Naw."

"*Naw naw naw*," Jech mocks. "*That the doubt in ya soul or tha bugs in ya skull eatin' at yer brains ta keep ya from figurin'?*" He stomps three times. A laser scans him and a door opens to a shuttle bay with a one-man craft. There's a transparent panel on the wall of the shuttle bay with nothing but space behind it. "Believe me now?"

Crim's ever still though his lack of a response is suggestive enough.

"I gotta be going." Jech tips an invisible brim of an invisible hat. "These rockets are about to kick into *hyper-drive*... Or something. Once that happens, you'll be in the sun in a matter of minutes."

He's exiting when something catches his attention. It's Crimson's eyes. They've gone from dead slate to fire.

With a look of pure determination, our psycho Sampson starts smashing his head into his chain-wrapped shoulders. Glow. Faster and faster and faster he goes. Chains stay tight but the glow intensifies.

"What do you think you're doing?" Jech asks out of curious concern.

Captive slows the masochism a second. He speaks but punctuates each word that coincides with each bash of his head. "We're in the vacuum of space *JECH*. Where'ya think the *ENERGY* required to heal *ME* is gonna *COME FROM*?" He goes back to pulverizing himself at a thousand miles an hour. *SMASH!* Glow intensifies as parts of the backyard scenario begin to dematerialize.

"Crim in containment unit!" Jech shouts.

SMASH!

Containment unit tries to materialize only to dissipate right back away as more of the blackhole scenario blinks out.

SMASH! SMASH!

"Too late!" Crim sings.

SMASH!

Now the whole damn scenario is blinking in and out, looking like a TV screen losing signal. Headbanging keeps on... *SMASH!* ...All while Jech hesitates, figuring. The chains around Crim lose several pixels *a* bash. His left arm's free. He ups the self-abuse. He flogs himself with that arm. Chunks fall from the parts of the black hole bare of any scenario. Right arm's free! Greater abuse, greater glow. *BLIP!* The whole scenario blinks out for good freeing Crim completely. He runs to the wall and drives his face into it. *BASH! BASH! BASH!*

What's hurting the structure more, Crim's blows or The

Gimmick? Either way, Jech's gotta stop it or they're all star junk.

SMASH!

"You'll blow us both into space!"

"Then come over hear and try ta stop me brotha." *SMASH!* "Could always use your gimmick too!" More chunks fall. Whole slabs of The Black Hole wall are dropping off now, revealing the shuttle hull behind it.

Jech continues running his calculus. Frantic. Nothing... Nothing... *Shuttle Bay!*

BAY'S CRUMBLING TOO. MOST CONCERNING is the viewing panel cracking to hell. He surveys the escape bay and all its contents. What exactly does he hope to find? Brick and mortar? A fire truck's worth of Flex Seal?

There's nothing here Jech. I'd tell you to ask the Black Hole for a copy of 'Repair Your Own Holodeck and Save' but here we are... Outta time asshole. Just what did you think—

Look!

A nuclear radiation emblem on the escape shuttle beams at him!

JECH RETURNS, RUSHING TO CRIM'S demolition. Hands are behind his back. Crim acts preoccupied though the second Jech's within reach, villain swings a powerful straight at him. *POP!* We see what was behind back because what was behind's now in front. A shuttle energy core. Crim's punched right through it!

SQUAWK! A mechanical voice issues from the shuttle bay,

Core rupture. Substantial radiation leak.

"All the energy you'll ever need," Jech sneers.

Crim tries pulling his hand out of the core but it won't budge. He goes back to pulverizing himself. No better. Glow funnels to a point aimed directly at the energy core. He's drawing energy from it and nothing else. He turns to Jech with that fire. He growls. This fuckin' guy actually growls...

"No!!!"

He's lost it. He's lost.

Fourth phase velocity increase in 30 seconds.

"Hope you brought your sunblock asshole!" Jech hoofs Crim in the gut so hard he sends him flying into the opposite wall near-instantly. Hits it with a *CRUNCH!*

At the *CRUNCH!*, the viewing panel of the shuttle bay bursts. The vacuum pressure wrenches the two men toward the breach like they're the next numbers in the Powerball. Shuttle bay seals automatically. Panels are half closed by the time Jech gets to them.

CRACK!

His feet go through the gap but his upper-body hits the closed portion of the doorway. He's hung up on it for a half-second before... *SCHLOOP!* The rest of him's sucked through the remaining:

Six...

Five...

Four inches of the opening.

Door seals just in time to stop Crim.

He hits it with another *CRUNCH!*

Glow.

He lays in a heap.

. . .

SILENCE. STILLNESS. THEN…

JECH BURSTS out the craft tumbling off into space. He's perpendicular the rocket's glare just as its hyper-drive after-burners kick in. Glare intensifies. The craft picks up so much speed so fast it zips out of sight instantly.

ROCKET'S MOVING FASTER THAN IT can maintain its own integrity. The fact that it's rapidly approaching the sun isn't helping either. Hull starts to crumble.

Crimson's still sitting slumped against the shuttle bay door, energy core still attached at his wrist. He's near perfectly still. The only discernible look on his face is… *Defeat*. What remains of The Black Hole dome is tearing away as we leave him.

THE CRAFT'S DISINTEGRATING LIKE A banana peeling. The material vaporizes into nothing as it rips away. The material blown off the craft moves away at a constant rate of acceleration in the half-second between detachment and atomization. All material except Crim… He's tumbling toward the star faster and faster. Maybe there's a glow coming off him but we're next to the sun here…

In short order the shuttle's completely vaporized. All we have left is Crim's little body streaking toward the star, soon to be a slave to its gravity. He continues streaking toward until…

A small surface flair.

Psst!

Toast.

· · ·

HE CAN'T SEE THE MOON. He can't see the Earth. Most importantly, he can't see Crimson. He saw the rocket craft kick into hyper-drive or something and fly off in the direction of the sun. Just as planned. He smiles. However, it's a smile that takes shape very slowly. He's cold, can barely move. He's simultaneously glowing and blue. It's an interesting shade.

We watch as the blue displaces The Gimmick. He's freezing more and more, freezing cryogenic until nothing left of life is apparent. He drifts, absolute zero, off into deep space. He's still. There's a look of peace. He's just another heavenly body now.

THE REMAINING INTERVENTIONISTS CIRCLE AROUND The Professor's equipment. Professor scans a monitor readout.

"Shuttlecraft at target destination."

"Is Crim in the oven?" asks Nand.

"I don't know," is the response. "I've lost contact with Jech." Professor moves to another monitor and pores over the information it provides. He's showing concern. Concern contingent on an answer. He gets it. "*No...*"

Simmons knows the tone, "What?"

He isn't responding.

"*What*?" she asks, more adamant.

He looks up to her with a welling in his eyes. Welling brings out a near imperceptible glow. She knows what that means too. She's only ever seen it in one other person her whole life and she knows what that means. Knows damn well.

The Professor rehearses what he's just read in the report, "*Escape shuttle inoperable.*"

"Then where's Roger?"

"I don't know."

She reaches to her lower abdomen, caresses, soothes? She can't hide the grief, "What do you mean you don't know? He's... He..." Anger tries to fill the vacuum left by grief only anger's early. Grief hasn't gone anywhere. Emotions congeal to blame. "Why'd you send him up there? Why? You son of a bitch! You should have told him no! You all should have told him not to go!" She pleads, "You have to bring him back."

Professor's head lowers. Nand and Etty comprehend. Tears fall of a pain too great for any more glow. "It's deep space. I—I can't imagine a scenario—"

She erupts. "You always have an answer! You always have an answer for everything!" She's striking him. There's a glow on his upper-body but Simmons doesn't care. "He trusted you! He trusted you and... And the one time... The one time it matters..." He stops her before she can hurt herself.

She's still yet she implores him. It's in her eyes.

He shakes his head.

"Please Toll."

He puts a hand to her cheek. Wipes away tears. She senses he's only trying to lighten the blow. She's not wrong.

"Roger *was* the answer."

She collapses. He catches her, half embracing her. She hugs onto him, sobbing.

THE MAKESHIFT COMMAND UNIT IS in the process of being disassembled. The Professor is cleaning up his workstation. He's putting various pieces of technology into a crate. His mechanical man is slumped on a chair next to those crates. Nand and Etty are muscling gear. Simmons is at her laptop.

A look at her screen reveals she's concluding a written piece. Text reads,

His name was 'The Interventionist' and he stood between every monster and the world.

She blinks out some tears. Starts typing again, editing,

His name was Roger Jech and he stood between every monster and the world.

She closes her laptop just as Suit-Man shows up, boorish as ever.

"I'd like to thank you all for a job well done!"

This aggravates all, none more-so than The Professor. "Well done? We don't even know if we were successful."

"Whattaya mean?"

"We don't know if Crimson was on that rocket."

"Either way. Fuckin' guy's in deep space now. Not our problem anymore."

"We lost a friend up there," he reminds.

Suit's nonplussed, "Can't die, right? Maybe he'll be back. Like Halley's comet or some shit. Anyway, gotta go." He pats The Professor on the shoulder, real enthusiastic. A little glow. Suit reacts. "Oh! Forgot about that woo-ee shit! Bye bye."

Simmons looks disgusted. She opens her laptop. She has one more edit to make. She deletes the word 'stood'. Writes: s-t-...

The definitively factual and finished text now reads,

His name is Roger Jech and he stands between every monster and the world.

Laptop closes. Simmons' eyes close too. We're in her dark now, when...

PSSSEWWWWWWWW! A shrill screech is heard.

PSSSSEWWWWWWWWWW! WHAT WE SEE IS Simmons in the foreground, sitting with her laptop, looking sad. Over her left shoulder we see Suit-Man walking away in that unmistakable suit, with that unmistakably smug strut.

PSSSEWWWWWWW! Continues, then, *CRASH!*

Over her shoulder we see a fiery streak smash to the ground right on top of Suit-Man. A crater's made on impact and debris shoots up from it in all directions. Simmons and everyone else in the area run toward the rubble.

Dust clears around Simmons, The Professor, Nand, and Etty, as the four stare into the hole. A yellow glow lights them up. Jech lays at the bottom wearing nothing but a few of The Professor's bullet proof panels. It's confusion for all outside of that crater.

WE'RE BACK A FEW MINUTES in time, looking at Space-Jech frozen solid. He continues to drift, completely blue. Blue, blue, blue, but... A little of that tenacious yellow returns. The Glow returns to his right arm. There's slight movement. Movement to his face too or else we couldn't tell that Jech's pained by something. He inches along his right side, finding the object causing his annoyance. His head ratchets down to confirm what's in his hand.

Can of air duster.

He tries twisting his head around to see what's behind. Still too frosty. He can't see the Earth yet he's pretty sure it's back there. He points the spray nozzle in the opposite direction of home and gives it a spritz.

His velocity slows.

He gives it another spritz.

He comes to a stop.

He depresses the nozzle full blast, finger fixed on the trigger this time. He's moving backward.

JECH APPROACHES EARTH'S ATMOSPHERE.

JECH ENTERS EARTH'S ATMOSPHERE. LIGHTS up.

JECH STREAKS THROUGH THE EARTH'S atmosphere like a meteor.

PSSSEWWWWWWWW! CRASH!

WE'RE BACK ON SIMMONS, THE Professor, Nand, and Etty confused a last second. Then... Elation. The four jump into the pit. All but Nand embrace Jech. Nand looks on in as much admiration as is warranted. Simmons holds on the hardest. She plants one on him, long though nowhere near as long as later. *SMACK!* He pulls her closer with one hand as Etty's clasps onto the other. Glow. Jech nods at The Professor who's trying to appear dignified. (Come on! He's clearly pleased!).

The Woman, our newest interventionist and Jech's other half, stares into the crater, curious. Jech notices. "My new protégé," he says to The Professor. "I thought you said you'd tell me on your deathbed."

Professor smiles a wry smile, "And if that time ever comes, I'll tell you again."

He shakes his head, put's his free hand on The Professor's shoulder.

Professor puts one back.

EPILOGUE

Mentor and Mentee work in the cellar laboratory. Good as new. Jech's looking at Crim's old containment unit like all his work is done. Professor Notices. He'd like to let the man mentally ride off into the sunset, but...

"Remember our first day in that government lab?"

"Yeah." Tone is wary out of the gate.

"I said, *I've told you all my secrets*?"

"Yeah..." He turns to face The Professor. "Were you lying?"

"No."

"*But*?"

Professor relents, only kinda, "I have no more secrets to *tell* you. However, I have one more to *show* you."

Jech's hardly surprised. "Jesus. I gotta exhaust every word in the English language I wanna get a straight answer out of you... What is it?"

Prof holds up a finger. *First things first.* He pulls Jech into the center of the lab with him. He stomps *shave and a haircut.*

A panel below descends.

DIM FLUORESCENT LIGHT SHINES IN the corner of the room where the two stand. Light's only there to illuminate a large switch. The Professor puts his hands on it.

"Ready?"

"As I'll never be."

He cranks the switch up. Light everywhere.

Jech walks toward the now-lit scene. Apparently quite the spectacle by the look on his face.

"Oh... No..."

He's slack-jawed. He turns to The Professor. Professor has a *now, I know what you're thinking* expression...

It's row upon row upon row of containment units, every single one of them occupied. Male interventionists, female interventionists, all shapes and sizes, all races and creeds. As far as the eye can see it's interventionists just sleeping in their microwaves.

The Professor shrugs at Jech and, in the weakest of proposals... "Boom, peace and harmony?"

www.ingramcontent.com/pod-product-compliance
Lightning Source LLC
Chambersburg PA
CBHW031302120726
47906CB00003B/843